Moonbeams and Mistletoe

SURRENDERED HEARTS - BOOK FOUR

ROSIE CHAPEL

First printing 2023

ISBN: 978-0-6457084-1-7 (ebook)
ISBN: 978-0-6457084-2-4 (Paperback)

Ulfire Pty. Ltd.
P.O. Box 1481
South Perth
WA 6951
Australia

www.rosiechapel.com

Cover Designed in Canvas by R Norman
Images Courtesy: Canva, Period Images, and Deposit Photos.

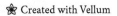 Created with Vellum

Acknowledgments

To…

Mum for her unfailing support, not to mention her eagle eye.

Melanie, whose encouragement keeps me going when I want to throw in the towel.

Dad for reading my books, even though they are not about Bomber Command!

Graham from Fading Street Publishing Services for his editing expertise.

My husband – the inspiration behind every one of my heroes.

My readers for coming on this journey with me. I truly appreciate your loyalty.

Thank you!

"Maybe sometimes, love needs a second chance because it wasn't ready the first time around."

Unknown

Moonbeams

and

Mistletoe

Chapter One

September 1819

E mily Livingston stood in the dappled shade of a huge beech tree, its leaves already beginning to turn, and observed the celebrations.

Ladies in shimmering gowns floated around the gardens chattering with their friends.

Men, attired in more sober hues, congregated in small groups, smoking pipes and discussing the state of the world.

Children darted about, their merriment echoing across the Radclyffe estate as they tumbled over each other, uncaring it was the ruination of their beautiful clothes.

A scene of joy.

A scene which made Emily's heart ache.

She turned her back on the revelry and started to walk away.

"Emily…" The single word, drifting on the breeze, stopped her in her tracks. For a split second, she thought, yearned… no… *don't be ridiculous, Emily…* she buried the hope deep, deep down.

ROSIE CHAPEL

"Emily." It was Nathaniel, her twin. The fact she could mistake his voice for that of James had become a source of anguish and comfort. *Would this sense of loss ever diminish?* Plastering on a bright smile, she spun on her heel to face him.

"You should not be alone, Em. Come join us." Nathaniel studied his sister solicitously.

"I wish you every happiness, Nate, but 'tis time I took my leave. Let me disappear quietly, before I forget I am the daughter of a marquis. One might be forgiven for believing one's protracted absence would curtail the gossips.

"Regrettably, that has not proved to be the case, and I am not so vulgar as to be disrespectful to your guests on your special day. Go…" she wagged her fan at the festivities, "… find Juliette. I shall be fine. Papa will be ready to go home, I can use him as an excuse without seeming impolite."

She could see Nathaniel was torn. "Nate, it is your wedding day, do not neglect your bride."

"Juliette knows where I am. Apparently, I became a trifle distracted, and she sent me to find you. I think because of 'Tish and Lawrence, she recognises the signs." Juliette's younger brother and sister were also twins.

Emily gave a low chuckle. "She is far too good for you."

Nathaniel grinned, a twinkle appearing in his eyes. "You think I don't know that?" he paused. "Em… James would no—"

Emily blinked back sudden tears. *Not today.* "You think I don't know that?" she mimicked, and linked arms with her brother. "Walk with me to say my goodbyes."

An hour later, Emily and her father, Archibald Livingston — the Marquis of Deerhurst, were ensconced in the family coach trundling towards London. The afternoon was waning, shrouding the distant city in a golden haze.

"Papa, look." Emily drew her father's attention to the view beyond the carriage as they came to a rise. "Oh, to be able to capture that on canvas," she sighed, and propped her elbows on the narrow window ledge, chin on her fisted hands.

Hearing an odd note in his daughter's voice, the marquis looked at her sharply. "Is everything all right, my dear?"

"Do not fret, Papa." Emily avoided a direct answer.

Lord Deerhurst's absent-minded demeanour hid a shrewd mind, a trait he cultivated deliberately, as anyone who had tried to outwit him discovered — usually to their detriment.

"What is it, Emily?"

Emily glanced over her shoulder. "Naught for you to be concerned about." Turning away from the vista rolling past, she settled into the seat. "Some things are simply too acute a reminder of what should have been." A faint blush stole up her cheeks at the confession.

Her father stretched across to pat her knee. "I do not possess your mother's knack for subtlety, but life must go on Em. I know you loved James, but 'tis four, nearly five years since he was killed. You are in danger of becoming a recluse, which would be a travesty. You are too vibrant a spirit for that."

"I fear I do not know how."

"This from the girl who travelled halfway around Europe, explored ancient ruins, sailed down the Nile, rode camels, slept in a Bedouin encampment? Emily Livingston, you are a courageous woman. You are not being disloyal to your betrothed by daring to live.

"James would be devastated if he knew you continue to pine for him. By all means, hold him in your heart, in your

3

memory but, be careful memory does not supersede reality, for then you too are lost."

"Papa…" Startled, Emily stared at her father. He had never spoken to her so… candidly before.

"Emily, you are my only daughter, and I miss you."

"I have been home for months."

"Do not prevaricate." His bushy brows furrowed. "Now, I have said my piece, just think on it."

The marquis changed the subject and, for the remainder of the journey, steered their conversation to frivolous topics, diverting Emily with some of his tales. Tall, they might have been, but they had the desired effect.

Emily did not forget his words.

That night, lying in her bed, Emily took stock and, after a lot of soul searching, concluded — to her pique — Papa was right. So, she had lost someone; she was not the only one. Hundreds, nay thousands of men had fallen in the recent wars alone, robbing wives of their husbands, children their fathers, mothers their sons, and sisters their brothers.

Loss was an unavoidable part of life, no one was immune. Although not much more than a child when her own mother passed away, Emily knew her father had been shattered, but somehow, surrounded by the love of his family, he found the strength to carry on. An example she would do well to emulate.

She, who had not thought twice about boarding a ship to lands unknown, who had trekked to remote sites, toured foreign cities, and tasted exotic cuisine was hiding behind a cloak of grief.

Emily shook her head.

"James is dead," she said out loud. "He was killed in battle. He died to protect his country. He died to protect me. Honour him by embracing every moment, by proving his sacrifice was worth it."

She summoned up his face in her mind. It was beginning to fade, but his features were still compelling. His eyes, blue as cornflowers, always sparkled when they fell on her. His dark hair reminiscent of ripe chestnuts. His toe-curling smile. His beautiful voice, which never failed to soothe her, no matter her disquiet.

His favourite phrase popped into her head, eliciting a reluctant grin. *All we need is moonbeams and mistletoe.* A nonsensical expression, but one spoken with the conviction it would fix everything.

"Yes, it sounds naive, but I have to believe, if we are part of a universe where moonbeams and mistletoe exist, nothing is insurmountable, for otherwise, what it the point?" he had said, when first she quizzed him about it.

"You are a dreamer, James," she had teased. "The world is not that simple."

"Oh, my dear, I think you will find, in essence, it is." He had swept her into his arms and kissed her until, as far as she was concerned, moonbeams and mistletoe could rule Britain.

"Thank you, James, for loving me," she murmured and, by sheer effort of will, let him go.

Chapter Two

October 1819

In the month since Nathaniel's wedding, Emily endeavoured to cast off the shell, she was unaware she had constructed around herself. Loyal friends coaxed her into attending one or two musical evenings and afternoon teas, ribbing her gently about her reclusive existence.

Thankfully, as it was between Seasons and many of the *ton* had retired to their country estates, social gatherings were scarce. Emily had been out of circulation for so long, adjusting to the unrestrained chatter of a gaggle of women proved rather a trial. They sounded like a flock of geese, all talking at once, no one listening. It was amusing, if somewhat headache inducing.

Neither was she ready to justify her extended sojourn. One day, she might feel inclined to share her adventures, but not yet. People were quick to judge, and she had no intention of allowing narrow-minded do-gooders to tarnish what had been an incomparable expedition.

After James' death, Emily had discovered her relatively

solitary existence, away from the edicts of Society was a balm. No one to answer to, no routine to follow, no tedious rules, no need to worry that accepting an invitation to Lady So-and-So's ball might offend Lady Such-and-Such, and it was hard to relinquish the autonomy associated therewith.

Neither was she in a hurry to do so. Cushioned by the love and patience of family and friends, hers would be a gradual thaw.

Likewise, in her determination to pick up the threads of her life, Emily, always an early riser, resumed her habit of taking a long constitutional before breakfast.

To tread empty pathways in the pearlescent dawn light, to watch the sun kiss the world awake and imbue the land with life-giving warmth was a privilege granted to a select few.

Here in London, it was bestowed on the merchants, the lamplighters, the birds... and her.

The mornings were noticeably cooler. Autumn was nigh. Trees showed hints of the glorious display with which they were about to dazzle. The swallows had massed and taken flight for southern climes. Small creatures were preparing for a long hibernation. The brilliant blue of the summer sky had taken on a paler hue, and the air a slight haze.

On the front step of Deerhurst Lodge, Emily breathed deeply, and an unexpected sense of well-being washed over her, lifting her spirits. Buttoning her ageing, but oh-so-comfortable, forest green redingote, she strode out towards Hyde Park... a favourite haunt.

She had been walking for perhaps half an hour when the peace was shattered by high-pitched squeals and the unmistakeable patter of fast-moving shoes. A grin twitched at her lips. There was nothing quite like the uninhibited exuberance of children.

Prudently, Emily stepped to the edge of the path, presuming — correctly as it happened — that she might get bowled over if she stayed where she was.

Two children, a boy, and a girl... so alike they *had* to be brother and sister... hurtled around the bend and charged full pelt towards her. Following in their wake, a harassed-looking girl of, Emily surmised, about ten and five years — the beleaguered nursemaid no doubt.

Before Emily could adjure the duo to slow down or risk a tumble, that very thing happened. As so often is the case with children, coordination between brain and body detached.

The little girl misstepped and, with a dramatic shriek, stumbled into her brother. Valiantly, he tried to steady them both, but their combined speed and weight made it impossible, and the pair careened into Emily.

All three ended up in a tangled heap on the damp grass.

"Lawks, what am I to do with you two?" The older girl huffed to a stop. "Bad enough you've likely ruined your clothes, but now you've squashed this poor lady."

The children clamoured that it was not their fault: the path was bumpy, their shoes were slippery, the birds were singing, and the sun was in their eyes. As the two scrambled to their feet, all manner of excuses tripped over their lips as fast as they had tripped over each other.

"Sorry, nice lady, we did not mean to knock you flying." The boy bowed, his shock of dark hair falling forward almost sweeping the grass.

"Are you hurt?" his sister asked anxiously, canting her head to study Emily.

"I do believe nothing is broken." She wriggled her arms, then stretched out her legs and flexed her feet in their sturdy boots. "There is only one problem…" Emily tapped her chin as though pondering a conundrum.

"What?" whispered the little girl, wide-eyed.

"How do I get up?"

The children looked at each other, then goggled at her open-mouthed, their matching expressions of panic prompting a gurgle of mirth to bubble up Emily's throat. She tried to stifle it, but even contorting her face into a hideous grimace — to the consternation of the three in front of her — it was a lost cause and she burst out laughing.

Her small audience gawked at this extraordinary reaction, but Emily's hilarity was contagious, and the children forgot to be alarmed, chortling merrily. Even the nursemaid's exasperation gave way to giggles at the ridiculous sight.

Eager to help, the two children offered Emily a hand. Eminently capable of getting to her feet without assistance, she allowed them to haul her upright. She brushed down her skirts, glad she was wearing one of her outdated gowns, now sadly crumpled and, as was her coat, marred by several muddy smears.

"Oh, my lady your clothes," the nursemaid fretted.

"Please do not think on it…" Emily's tone lifted in a tacit question.

"Jenny, miss, my lady," that young lady supplied, with a neat curtsy.

"…Jenny. No harm done." She smiled at the flustered nursemaid. "'Tis good for children to let off some steam now and again."

"Every morning, my lady," Jenny replied with an exaggerated eye roll.

"I imagine an hour of running around the park settles them for the rest of the day," Emily postulated.

"If only. Oh, beggin' your pardon, my lady, I didn't mean to speak out of turn. They are a lively pair and no mistake, and gracious, they can get up to mischief. I need eyes in the back of my head, but there's no badness in 'em."

"How old are they?"

"Nearly five."

Emily chuckled. "A good age for getting into scrapes. I too am a twin and recall running amok with my brother. It is refreshing to see children being children. They will be constrained soon enough."

Two sets of ears pricked up at Emily's remark.

"You are a twin?" the boy interjected.

"I am." She smiled down at his inquisitive face.

"What is your name?" his sister demanded.

"Minnie," Jenny chided, "manners."

"Sorry." A frown flitted across Minnie's brow, and she blew a sigh. "It is hard to 'member all the rules."

Emily crouched so she was eye level with the child. "I agree, but the more you use them, the easier they become. I still make mistakes."

"You do?" Minnie's eyes grew round again.

"All the time. So let us practice some now. I am Lady Emily Livingston." She sank a curtsy.

A perky smile dimpling her cheeks, Minnie copied Emily, wobbling when she dipped her knees. "I am pleased to make your 'quaintance. I am Lady Minnie Barth'mew."

"I am Lord Matthew Bartholomew," the little boy enunciated every syllable in the surname slowly, shooting a disdainful glance at Minnie. "Earl of Wharton," he finished, puffing his chest out importantly.

"My, my, your lordship, it is an honour to meet you." Emily hid a grin behind her hand and dropped another curtsy.

"I do not know what an earl is, but Papa says I do not have to worry about that yet," Matthew inched closer to mutter confidentially.

"Your Papa is correct. You will not have to think about being an earl for years and years. Plenty of time to chase around the park," she reassured, then turned to his sister. "Might I ask what Minnie is short for?"

"Minerva." Minnie beamed.

"The Roman goddess of, hmmm… let me see, wisdom, poetry, courage, and justice, oh lots of wonderful things. A venerable name. As is Matthew," she hastened to add.

Minnie clapped her hands and pirouetted on her toes. "Papa said that too, but I like Minnie better."

"You have the best of both worlds. Minnie is perfect for now, and you can decide whether you prefer Minerva when you are older."

"How do *you* know about Roman goddesses?" Matthew chimed in.

"Hmmm, I think I was about your age when I began to read about them. We had, still have I believe, a great big book about myths and legends. I loved it."

"May we visit them?" Minnie asked optimistically.

"Silly, they are not real," Matthew scoffed. "Just make-believe."

Minnie scowled and folded her arms.

Sensing a squabble brewing, Emily intervened, "A long time ago, gods and goddesses were thought to control a person's life and the world in which they lived. A way to explain things they could not understand, like the weather, or the seasons, or sickness. People revered them hoping, in return, these gods would show them favour… errr… would be kind to them," she amended seeing confusion on the twins' faces.

"Bit like when we pray in church," Jenny said helpfully.

"Have you met one?" This from Minnie.

"Even had they existed, I am not that old." Emily chuckled. "Although I have seen statues of some. Minerva was very beautiful."

"Ohhhhhhhhh, where did you see her?" Minnie was more interested in whether she too could see her namesake, than her appearance.

"In Rome."

"Where's that?"

"Italy, a country three weeks from England, by ship."

Chapter Three

E mily's disclosure sparked a flurry of questions, which Jenny tried to stem — with negligible effect, it must be admitted.

"We ought to be going home. Your father will think we have got lost," she said.

"We want to hear about Rome," Matthew wheedled.

"If we do not go now, you will miss breakfast," Jenny coaxed.

Loath to interfere with Jenny's routine, Emily was also torn. Averse to making a commitment, something about the twins tugged at her — perhaps memories of her own childhood, when life was less… complicated.

Regarding their earnest faces and, against her better judgement, she offered a solution. "You say you come here every morning?" She looked at Jenny.

Jenny nodded.

"Might you be agreeable to meeting me here tomorrow, if 'tis clement, and I will tell you about Rome?"

"Please, please, pleeeeeeeeease," the twins beseeched, their faces the very definition of cherubic.

"You pair will be the death of me." Jenny's benevolent smile softening her admonishment. "Please thank Lady Emily for her kindness.

"Thank you, Lady Emily," they chorused with unabashed glee.

"My pleasure. I look forward to seeing you on the morrow. Be sure to behave for Jenny, or she may be tempted to change her mind." Emily winked at Jenny who smothered a giggle. "A little bribery never hurt," she murmured for Jenny's ears only.

In her wildest dreams, Emily could not have foreseen how far 'a little bribery' would lead.

Like clockwork, Emily met the trio every morning. Wrapped up warmly against the autumnal air, they found a bench near the Serpentine and, to the backdrop of waterfowl foraging amongst the reeds, Emily told tales of lands afar.

Minnie and Matthew listened agog, fascinated by her descriptions: of pyramids, vast rivers, and crocodiles, of gladiators, ancient ruins, and exploding mountains. They peppered Emily with questions about camels, deserts, and tents, cities built on canals, soaring basilicas, ships, and caravans.

Jenny was heard to murmur, she had never seen them so diligent, thrilled at how much they were learning without even trying. "As am I," she added. "Such wonders of this world. You are fortunate indeed to have witnessed them."

"I am blessed," Emily agreed. "The reason for my voyage, for my adventures, was to escape a grief from which I

14

thought I would never recover, and it became an experience unparalleled."

"I do not wish anyone sorrow, my lady, but 'tis glad I am you found solace in your travels and are willing to share them with us."

"To find eager listeners is a boon. My family is heartily sick of me talking about them." Emily gave a wry grin. "Now, have any of you heard of a sphinx?" She looked at the three, who stared at her baffled. "Oh, my dears..." and she entertained them with a description of the colossal cat-like sculptures, and other marvels of Egypt until it was time to part.

Emily watched the three as they left the park. Matthew and Minnie trotted alongside Jenny, their litany of questions wafted back to her on the breeze. Smiling, she tilted her face to the sun, basking in its meagre warmth.

In that moment, a frisson of happiness stole over her — an emotion she had not realised was missing, and a last glance at the retreating trio told her where lay the source.

She strolled home, a newly revived spring in her step.

Ascending the stairs on the way to his bedchamber, Henry Bartholomew, 6th Marquis of Stapleton, was distracted by the hubbub emanating from the nursery. The lively chatter persuaded his feet in that direction, and he strode along the carpeted hall to peer around the door.

Matthew and Minnie were sitting on the floor, playing with a selection of wooden toys. On the face of it, nothing out of the ordinary, but further observation revealed this was not a simple game. No, this involved a quest, which crossed the high seas to distant lands where they battled strange creatures.

While their geography was disastrously awry... and anyone trying to follow their trail would end up forever lost... the countries being named were no fantasy.

Henry frowned, *from where, or who, on earth had they garnered their knowledge?*

Minnie spotted him first. "Papa," she squealed in excitement. They rarely saw their father during the day. "Come and play, pleeeeeeeeease."

Jenny jumped up from her seat where she had been engrossed in darning yet another of Matthew's socks. "Minnie, your papa is a busy man. We must not interrupt his morning."

Henry raised a placatory palm. "Thank you, Jenny, but do not take on. I would be a sorry excuse of a father if I could not spare time for my children." He hunkered down next to the twins and picked up a fallen horse. "Pray tell, what is this game? 'Tis not one with which I am familiar."

"The H'explorations of an Earl and his Sister," Matthew entitled their romp. "We are on a..." he screwed up his face trying to remember how Emily had described it. "...a grand tour of the whole world."

"A grand tour? The whole world?" Henry clapped a hand to his chest and, instilling a note of mild consternation into his voice, declared theatrically, "You will be gone for months. How shall I manage without you?"

Giggling, Minnie leant against him. "Papa, you are funny. We are not acshully leaving home, 'tis pretend."

"*Pretend?*" Henry waggled his brows comically. "Oh, what a relief." He looped an arm around his daughter and hugged her.

Matthew handed his father a wooden knight. "This is

Lord Wharton," then a carving of a woman with a cat, "and this is Lady Minerva. They are on a ship, bouncing over the waves…"

"I was not sick," Minnie interrupted. "I have sea legs."

"…on their way from Rome to…"

"Athens…" Minnie screeched, nearly deafening Henry.

"Turkey," Matthew corrected loftily.

"No, Athens."

"Turkey."

"As you have to pass Athens on the way to Turkey," Henry felt it pertinent to intercede before their discussion deteriorated into a heated argument, a regular occurrence when Matthew tried to overrule Minnie, "might I advocate two stops? First Athens and then on to Turkey."

This shut the pair up while they pondered his suggestion.

"The ship's captain agrees," Matthew intoned.

"Goody." Minnie clapped. "What's an Athens?" she cocked her head at Henry enquiringly.

Henry chuckled. "It is the capital of Greece. No, not geese, Greece," reading Minnie's puckered forehead accurately. "There are lots of old and, I believe, beautiful buildings. It is possible to view some of the sculptures in the museum. Greece is where, legend tells us, the gods and goddesses live."

"Have you seen them?" Matthew asked.

"No, they are, in the same way as your story, pretend. Like the characters in fairy tales."

"Please tell us?" Minnie chimed in.

"Perhaps tonight at bedtime." Henry sought to avert.

"Lady Emily knows about them *all*," Minnie said. "She's been everywhere. *She* prob'ly had tea with them."

That snagged Henry's undivided attention. *Lady Emily? Was this another figment of their vivid imaginations*. "Is Lady Emily aboard ship with you? Your chaperone perhaps?"

Matthew chortled and shook his head at his father's question. "Papa, we have Jenny."

Jenny, the hole sewn up neatly, confessed quietly, "Lady Emily is a lady whom we... errr... chanced upon in the park. Generously, she has been telling the twins about her travels."

Henry looked over the children's heads at Jenny, who felt her cheeks burn. "A lady in the park?" His tone quizzical.

"Papa, she is so pretty," Minnie spoke before Jenny could reply. "She knows what my name means, and that Minerva was a Roman goddess... oh..." another thought struck her. "I 'spect she has taken tea with her too." She nodded sagely, completely forgetting Emily's explanation as to why ancient folk invented the realm of the gods, and her father's grin resurfaced.

"Does Lady Emily have a surname?" he addressed this to Jenny.

"Livingston," Jenny supplied. "My lord, I would never place the twins in an untenable situation. Perhaps it seems odd to you that a lady would take the time to talk with children, but I think it brightens her day.

"Lady Emily appears," she cast about for the right word, "not sad as much as wistful and mayhap a trifle lonely, but she has given no indication of ill-intent and when she talks of her expedition, her face lights up, making me think the privations she must have endured, worth it.

"Certainly, she has visited many countries, and has gained a prodigious knowledge of their history and culture. I will say, my lord, she has renewed the children's interest in learning. They want to know everything I can teach them about the places Lady Emily has seen."

It was probably the longest speech Jenny had made to the marquis, praying he did not think her impertinent.

Apparently not. "Praise indeed," was all Henry said mildly.

"This woman sounds like quite the paragon. Mayhap I ought to meet her."

Jenny dipped her head, but forbore from commenting, assuming the question did not require an answer.

"Yes, yes, Papa, yes, we are going tomorrow…" Minnie implored.

To assuage his concerns by speaking to this Lady Emily was only a half-formed idea, but there was little Henry could deny his daughter when she was at her most winsome.

"Matthew, what say you?"

Matthew considered his father's question seriously. "If you promise to be good, we should be pleased for you to come with us."

"I am always good," Henry defended himself.

Two pairs of grey eyes fixed him with identical indulgent stares.

"I am," he protested, swinging Minnie into his arms to tickle her mercilessly, making her shriek with laughter.

Shortly thereafter, frivolity echoing in his brain, Henry left them to their day.

Briefly, he pondered the mystery of Lady Emily, but she was soon pushed to one side, the duties of the day taking precedent.

Tomorrow would be here soon enough.

Chapter Four

The following morning dawned cool and overcast, although hints of pale blue could be discerned through the sulky grey clouds. On the doorstep, Emily hugged her cloak around her, chosen for warmth rather than fashion.

"It looks a mite bleak, Lady Emily," Mr Walters, the Livingston's butler, worried.

"Perfect autumn weather, Mr Walters," Emily replied. "Just right for a stroll around the park. I doubt the twins will be there this morning, but I am savouring my constitutionals." Given her attire had required cleaning after her ignominious tumble, the household knew all about Matthew and Minnie.

"There'll be a hot breakfast ready for your return." Mr Walters held the door. "Mind you don't get chilled."

Emily grinned at the elderly retainer, who still treated her like the heedless child she used to be. "I shall take every care." She ran lightly down the steps, turning to wave as she struck out along the path.

Moments later, after dodging lamplighters, window

cleaners, and the odd vendor's cart, she was in the relative peace of the park. She could hear the faint drum of hooves in the distance; someone enjoying an early ride.

Once an everyday pastime, it was one she had yet to resume, in the main because it kindled too many memories. James and she had ridden together as often as possible, precious hours away from Society's eagle eyes. Rebellious… perhaps… but worth the raised brows.

Resolutely, Emily pushed the ripple of melancholy aside and took the path towards the bench the quartet had adopted as theirs. The squawking of waterfowl a sure sign the twins — unperturbed by the dreary weather — had beaten her here, and were already tossing crumbs, begged from their cook, for the hungry birds.

She quickened her pace, coming to an abrupt standstill when she saw a well-dressed man, crouched next to Minnie, holding a paper bag while she scattered scraps to the four winds.

She studied the two heads bent together.

The stranger was smiling at the little girl who chattered incessantly. This must be their father. *Was he here to scold, or…?*

All of a sudden, the anticipation of a light-hearted inter-lude, of a cosy gossip with Jenny, mixed with the enjoyment of storytelling, fled. Normally prepared, nay willing to act with reckless disregard for the consequences, in this, Emily faltered.

She did not want Lord whatever his name was to think she was interfering in the lives of his children — perhaps she ought to have requested permission before spinning yarns… however truthful.

Had she overstepped an archaic and hitherto invisible bound-ary? Emily scoured her brain for an answer, coming up blank.

Unwilling to intrude, she spun around intent on leaving unseen, forgetting the gravel, which grated under her heel.

"Em'ly."

She heard Minnie's yell, but paid no heed, and increased her pace.

"Lady Emily Livingston?" a deep voice called.

Emily didn't acknowledge that either.

There came the rapid pad of small feet and a mittened hand slipped into hers, halting her flight.

"Em'ly," Minnie reproached. "Why are you going? Papa came today 'spesh'ly."

Reluctant to upset the child, Emily swithered. "I... err... mayhap..."

By now the man had joined them.

"Papa, this is Emily. I told you she was pretty." Minnie jigged up and down, thrilled at being the one to make the introductions.

Hectic colour stained Emily's cheeks, as she met the attentive gaze of the twins' father. Covering her embarrassment, she dipped a curtsy.

"My lord," she greeted.

"Henry Bartholomew, Marquis of Stapleton, at your service." The man bowed. "My children have not stopped lauding your talents as a storyteller, and I confess I was intrigued to meet the person who has inspired their recent zest for lessons." His voice lifted in slightly cynical question.

"Lord Stapleton, please accept my sincerest apologies. I had no mind to usurp the routine of your household, or cause offence. It began as a way to distract Lord Wharton and Lady Minerva following a... an... accidental encounter and, I admit it was flattering to have an avid audience." Emily tried to justify.

"I realise I am a stranger, although, I suspect you will have heard of my family, and understand should you prefer me not to continue my... err... our... conversations."

Henry studied the young lady as she spoke, noting — absently — one or two glossy brown ringlets peeking out from under her hat, pink cheeks, and apprehensive eyes, eyes the colour of richly brewed coffee. *Richly brewed coffee... Henry Bartholomew what are you thinking?* He coerced his recalcitrant brain back to the matter at hand.

"Fret not, Lady Emily." His raised hand forestalling Emily's rush of words. "I am pleased to make your acquaintance." He vacillated a moment, then decided on honesty.

"I confess the reason for my attendance this morning is because I am concerned. Not only does it seem my children are badgering a poor unsuspecting victim, but also, said victim is regaling them with tales which sound... to the casual ear... extraordinary."

"You wish to ascertain whether I am fabricating stories for some fiendish reasons of my own. Perhaps gaining their trust in order to steal them away to hide them in my shoe, or lock them in my gingerbread house?"

Emily spoke half in jest and half in challenge. While she appreciated and accepted the man's compulsion to check on this unusual gathering, her affront that he questioned her motives was not easily quashed. "If t'will ease your mind, the Marquis of Deerhurst would gladly vouch for my character." Her chin went up.

Henry, cognisant of nursery rhymes and contes de fées — some of which he could recite backwards, to his own chagrin — swallowed a grin at Emily's allusion. He was about to respond when Minnie, wise beyond her years, sensed undercurrents and, determined her Papa would *not* spoil their fun, interrupted.

Hands on hips, she stamped her foot. "Papa, this is not a fairy tale and Em'ly is not a nasty witch. She is our friend."

Henry raised a brow at Emily who met his gaze guilelessly — a warning sign if ever he saw one.

Crouching until he was eye level with his daughter, he reassured, "I do not think Lady Emily is in any way wicked, poppet, but it is my job as your father to protect you, and that means it is important I know with whom you are spending your time when not at home."

Minnie skewered her father with a hard stare. "May Em'ly keep telling us about her a'ventures?"

Henry sent up a silent prayer that his intuition was not awry. "She may."

"Promise?"

"My word of honour."

"Goodie." Squishing her father's cheeks between her gloved hands, Minnie kissed him. "Thank you. Matthew," she trilled, scampering over the grass to her brother. "We can play with Em'ly foooorevaaah."

"Goodie," Matthew echoed Minnie's approval. "Here," he handed her some breadcrumbs and, consigning the adults to the background, the pair focused on the ducks.

Jenny, glad the master had no objections to their arrangement, sent Emily a bright smile and turned her attention to the children who were likely to fall into the Serpentine in the excitement of feeding the birds.

Henry straightened up and inclined his head towards the bench. "Are you brave enough to sit with me?" he invited, a hint of the smile he bestowed on Minnie, softening sombre features.

Emily blinked at the transformation and, ignoring the peculiar sensation it caused, nodded her agreement.

An awkward silence descended as they watched the children hopping about, one Emily felt unable to break, despite a question hovering on the periphery of her mind. A point of etiquette which *had* to be addressed before they could discuss anything other than the vagaries of the weather.

As far as she knew, Lord Stapleton was a married man.

In the short time since meeting the twins, it had become clear, if they had a mother, she did not reside in the city. Neither was the woman mentioned... ever — not even in an aside.

While several reasons for this peculiar absence presented themselves, until Emily knew which was correct, associating with someone else's husband, however innocently, was one rule she would never flout.

She was scrabbling for a polite way to phrase what bothered her when Lord Stapleton spoke.

"So, Lady Emily, I understand you are well-travelled."

"I believe I am," Emily hedged, pestered by the notion this man was trying to throw her off balance... figuratively speaking.

He persevered. "If it is not too bold a question, what prompted such an adventure?"

"If it is not too bold a reply, may I ask whether our conversation is appropriate?"

Henry was at a loss. "I beg your pardon?"

"My lord, I may be past my majority, but I remain unwed. This," she gestured between them, "is treading a fine line, and I have no intention of being discourteous, or..." she watched Henry's brows knit in visible confusion.

She stopped beating about the bush.

"My lord, what of your wife?"

In any other circumstance, the relief which swept over

Henry's face would have been comical. "Oh, my lady, forgive me. I thought you knew. My wife died several years ago."

"Oh," That took the wind from Emily's sails, and she sagged against the wood of the bench. "I am so sorry. I did not mean to rake up the past... must be so painful..." she trailed off, mortified by her gaffe.

"There is naught to apologise for. It was not unexpected, and she lives on in our children." Henry did not elaborate, and Emily had absolutely no intention of prying.

Notwithstanding her camaraderie with the twins, their father remained a stranger, and one did not reveal personal details to strangers, however handsome they were.

That sent the heat back up her cheeks colouring them bright red and she swallowed a groan.

Hiding a grin at Emily's discomfiture — although clueless as to the reason — Henry, with an adroitness honed from years of being on parliamentary committees, steered the conversation back to the original topic.

"Now 'tis clear you are not breaching any rules, might you disclose why you decided to travel the world?"

Chapter Five

E mily leant against the back of the bench to stare up at the leaden sky, letting the autumnal air cool her hot cheeks.

"A change was imperative, I required time away from everything familiar, from the rules, and the conventions. Perhaps…" she stopped.

It was obvious there was more, and Henry, detecting a note of melancholy in her voice, wondered at the cause. "Generally, people retire to the country or visit the coast for the duration, not board a ship and circle the globe. Yours was a courageous alternative." Hoping to elicit a smile, although for why eluded him, he injected a hint of humour into his remark.

Emily glanced at him, expecting censure, to see naught but genuine interest.

"Our world is awash with marvels. The majority about which, under normal circumstances, I would have remained unenlightened." She heard herself and huffed a sigh.

"Forgive me. I did not mean to sound pompous. In truth, it was cowardice not courage precipitated my decision. I was running away, escaping from what, at the time, seemed unassailable.

"Fortunately, it was a decision I do not regret, and became an experience beyond imagination. I was inspired by my great aunt who used to tell us children of her Grand Tour, and decided if she could do it, so could I. It was definitely grand, but oddly, it was also a pilgrimage, a voyage of discovery… about me as much as the phenomena I beheld.

"Yes, there were risks, dangers, but they paled into insignificance when compared with the magical sights, the sounds, the smells — the fragrant, and the distinctly malodorous…" she pulled a wry face. "The people, the diverse cultures, and the history… oh the history."

She blushed again. "You will be sorry you broached this subject. As you can see, I tend to get carried away, just ask your children."

"On the contrary, Lady Emily, I am riveted, and in the same spirit, might I pose a question?"

Not entirely sure where this was leading, Emily inclined her head, noncommittally.

"While my proposition is somewhat… unconventional and definitely bends those rules you once tried to evade, I find myself keen to hear more about your travels. Would you object to me accompanying these two rapscallions when my commitments permit, of course."

"Errr… you want to spend time with us? Before breakfast?" Emily blurted out in astonishment.

"I have been known to take an occasional stroll on an empty stomach," he replied dryly. "Lady Emily, studying geography and history in a classroom, while interesting, lacks… flair. Nothing more than words on a page. I have spent time beyond our shores, but those days are best forgotten. To see the continent through your eyes, might repaint the picture in a brighter palate."

Aware to what he referred, Emily smiled sympathetically and, without thinking, patted his hand. "My lord, if you are willing to rise with the birds just to listen to my prattle, I do not see how I can possibly object."

And so, it began.

November 1819

Deeming it prudent not to appear too eager, Henry waited until the following week before he escorted the trio on their early morning walk. The weather had turned wintry, and a dusting of frost made the paths slippery.

Matthew and Minnie skipped along, their garrulous chatter masking the fact, the two adults were silent.

Jenny was tongue-tied, unwilling to start a conversation with the master of the house. *What could she talk about anyway?*

Deep in thought, Henry had not noticed her reticence.

They reached the bench and Jenny heaved a sigh of relief. Emily was already there, standing by the water's edge, her dark red cloak a cheerful splash of colour against the stark landscape.

"Em'ly," Minnie bellowed, oblivious to her father's wince, and dashed across the grass.

Smiling, Emily caught Minnie in a hug, and twirled her around.

"Oh, I'm a bird," Minnie crowed.

"Me too, me too." Matthew stretched out his arms.

Laughing, Emily stood Minnie on the ground, ensuring she was not going to tipple over. "Do you think me strong enough to spin around a young man of your stature?" she teased.

Face scrunched up, Matthew pondered the question seriously. Standing beside Emily, he placed his hand on the top of his head and measured his height against her. "I 's'pect so. See, I'm not thaaaaat big."

"You asked for it." Emily clasped his waist and whisked him into the air, his delighted yells echoing around the lake.

"Matthew, you will wake the dead." Despite the early hour and lack of people in the vicinity, Henry thought it wise to curb his son's enthusiasm — to no discernible effect.

Emily set Matthew on his feet and shooed him off to his sister and Jenny. Slightly dizzy, the boy reeled like a drunken sailor, making everyone giggle.

Sobering, and unaccountably shy, Emily dipped a curtsy. "Good morning, my lord."

"Good morning, Lady Emily. I trust you are well." Henry removed his topper and bowed.

"Thank you, yes."

"Perhaps a prom…"

"Might you be amen…"

They spoke in unison, stopped, took a breath, and started again, still talking over each other.

Emily felt hilarity simmering and, staring at the path, bit her lip to suppress it.

She heard an odd sound and glanced up to see Henry was equally amused.

"This is ridiculous. We are intelligent adults, yet the art of conversation seems to have abandoned us. Were any of my brothers here, they would fall over themselves in their hurry to warn you, I am an inveterate chatterbox."

Henry sensed an opening. "Your brothers, tell me of them."

"There is little to tell, save Nate, my twin—"

"You are a twin? I am sorry, I did not mean to interrupt."

"Yes, and he married into a family with another set of twins. Twins, it seems are, everywhere." She grinned unself-consciously and, like the dawn's mist under the morning sun, the inexplicable tension between them evaporated.

"I have two more brothers, Michael and Gareth, both married with children."

"You are the only daughter?"

"I am and, although I always wanted a sister, growing up with three brothers was... hmmm — how best to describe it? — entertaining. My mother despaired I would ever master the grace and poise expected by Society." Emily canted her head in thought. "That said, I believe, secretly, she was proud of my ability to wield a sword, fire a gun, and ride bareback."

Henry could not help it. "Fire a gun?" he croaked.

"Useful skill when travelling lands afar," Emily quipped with studied nonchalance.

An image of Emily in piratical garb popped into Henry's head. Interestingly, it suited her. Emily was speaking; he banished the picture, with limited success, and forced himself to concentrate.

"Mama was a rare person." Emily's voice had assumed a faraway tone. "Family meant everything to her, and she ensured we grew up knowing her support for us was unequivocal. When anyone judged it pertinent to offer their *expert* opinion on our conduct, which they decreed as *unworthy of our status*," her lip curled cynically, "she listened politely but, despite giving every indication our transgressions would be dealt with accordingly, took no notice whatsoever.

"'Tis not to say we were allowed to behave like savages.

We were cognisant of the rules. It was simply that Mama knew how intimidating adulthood, with all its formalities, seemed and, she preferred us to enjoy our freedom for as long as practicable.

"Had she known of my plans, I posit she might have been tempted to accompany me on my travels or, at the bare minimum, while concerned for my safety, championed my decision."

Henry glanced at Emily whose eyes were shadowed. Despite his apparent ignorance of her family — a ploy to coax her into conversation — Henry Bartholomew, 6th Marquis of Stapleton, was not a man to do *anything* without garnering as much information about a situation — or in this case, person, as possible.

To this end, he had done his due diligence to ascertain everything he could about Lady Emily Livingston.

He knew her father was the Marquis of Deerhurst, clarifying her assertion, he would bear testament to her good standing, and that her mother had died almost two decades previously. He knew Nathaniel worked for Major Lucas Withers — a man with whom he was well acquainted.

He had rubbed shoulders with her oldest brother in the venerable halls of parliament, and had crossed paths with Gareth, briefly, during one of the last campaigns of the recent wars.

The necessity of ensuring his children were not being schooled into something nefarious, aside, Emily Livingston fascinated him. In some respects, she remained an enigma, unquestionably possessed of an indomitable strength, yet lurking behind her carefree façade, he sensed a fragility and was struck by a desire to be her bastion without extinguishing her hard-won liberty.

They had barely been introduced, to pry beneath the surface was discourteous, but her face reared up in his mind when he least expected, and the oddest notion he had known Emily all his life lingered.

Something stirred deep in his soul; an emotion long forgotten, one he did not recognise and, as such, he quashed it.

It refused to be denied.

Chapter Six

December 1819

I n a sizeable nursery, not far from Deerhurst Lodge, two children seemed intent on hindering their extremely patient maid's efforts to dress them appropriately.

The sun might be shining in a clear blue sky, but it was bitterly cold, and the city had awoken to a hard frost. Warm clothing was the order of the day, or there would be no walk.

"Stand still," Jenny exhorted, trying to button coats and fasten boots while the objects of her attention bounced around like marionettes on invisible strings.

"You are making me dizzy. 'Tis not for the good of *my* health you should wrap up. What has got into you this morning? Cats on hot coals are less boisterous." She shook a tolerant finger.

"We're going to see Em'ly," Minnie chanted, hopping on one leg.

Matthew marched in circles, swinging his arms military

style. "Jason and the Angonups… no… Artegoes…" his nose wrinkled in concentration. "Nagautons… no."

Giving up, Matthew plumped for, "Jason and his crew, go on an adventure to find something important. E m i l y," he pronounced each letter, shaking his head at Minnie, "promised to tell us the story."

"'Tis a legend," Minnie chimed in, not in the slightest chastened by her brother's patronising tone. "Hurry up, Jenny," she begged.

"If the pair of you had stopped your wild capers when I asked, we would have been there *hours* ago," Jenny exaggerated, her feigned exasperation ruined when the twins became rooted to the spot and assumed angelic expressions.

She smothered a chuckle. "Right my sweet cherubs, are you ready? Lady Minerva?"

"Ready," Minnie sang.

"Lord Matthew?"

Matthew responded with marginally less vigour.

"Hats, coats, boots, mittens." Jenny went through the list, smiling as the children waved or pointed at each article of clothing. "Finally. Come along you imps."

Her hand on the front door, Jenny recalled the little packet cook had saved.

"Faith! I nearly forgot the breadcrumbs… hmmm…" she rubbed her chin, thoughtfully. "Do you think the ducks will mind, just this once?"

It was an oft repeated question, and the same answer was forthcoming.

"Jenny, you *know* the ducks get very hungry and 'spect us to feed them." Minnie pinned Jenny with a penetrating gaze.

"Fine." Jenny continued the game. "'Tis not my fault if Lady Emily has not the time to tarry."

"Be quick, Jenny." Minnie danced a jig in encouragement.

Head full of a knotty problem, he and a select group of his parliamentary colleagues were trying to resolve, Henry Bartholomew came out of his study, papers in hand, to see his children, dressed for a walk, and no sign of Jenny.

Had he agreed to take them to the park this morning? Was Jenny otherwise engaged? Wracking his brain, Henry drew a blank, but had no mind to renege on a commitment, despite no recollection of making one.

He dropped the papers on a cabinet inside his study, then grabbed his greatcoat, thick scarf, and topper, which were hanging, conveniently, on the hatstand by the door.

"Onward, intrepid explorers," he said. A small hand slipped into each of his as the trio trooped out of the door and down the steps. Boots clicking crisply on the path, Henry set a brisk pace to stave off the chill air which turned their breath into tiny white clouds as they chattered.

They were scarcely out of sight when Jenny reappeared. Her return delayed when the breadcrumbs were not where she expected to find them. Flummoxed by the absence of two small children, she stood in the empty hall, at a loss. Where had they gone?

She ran upstairs, calling for the twins, to be met with silence. It was eerie. Opening the front door, she scanned the street both ways, expecting to see Minnie and Matthew skipping about on the cobbles.

They were nowhere to be seen.

Unnerved, she hurried through the baize door, on the off chance they had missed each other when she went upstairs. The twins were not there either.

"Surely they would not go to the park without me?" she asked out loud.

"Nothing would surprise me with that pair." Susie, one of the parlourmaids, grinned.

"Best you follow your usual route, I daresay you'll find them by the lake," Cook said comfortingly, rolling pastry.

"If they come back…" she dithered.

"We shall tie them to a chair." Mr Jarvis, the butler, chuckled. "Go on with you, lass, we'll watch out for them."

Jenny bolted.

Emily was astonished to see Jenny racing along the slippery paths, minus her usual charges.

"Are the twins unwell?" she quizzed as the young maid slithered to ungainly halt, gasping for breath.

"Have you seen them? Have you seen Minnie and Matthew?" Jenny wheezed.

"Seen them? Not a sign. Have you been playing hide and seek? Rascals." Emily turned in a slow circle, expecting the twins to appear, giggling at being able to trick Jenny.

Frantic, and hot from her mad dash, Jenny panted, "They have vanished."

"Vanished?" Emily stared at Jenny, a trickle of ice crawling down her spine — nothing to do with the frigid air.

"Children do not vanish, Jenny," she said bracingly, aware it was not unheard of, but unwilling to add to the nursemaid's alarm. "What happened?"

Jenny explained.

When she had finished, Emily reassured. "I cannot imagine they have gone very far and are certain to be within the park. 'Tis so close they probably imagined you would be right behind them. You know how easily they are distracted. We shall look for them together."

Emily's pragmatism calmed the panicked girl and, after precious minutes discussing the likely paths the children might follow, the two began to search.

They were methodical, hunting high and low, even checking copses and thickets in case the twins *were* playing hide and seek. It was almost an hour later, and Jenny was on the verge of tears, when a familiar chortle floated towards them on the still air.

Emily glanced at Jenny; both mouthed, "Minnie."

The sound led them to a sheltered corner where there stood a crumbling belvedere, its roof long gone and half-hidden by a riot of holly, laurel, and yew. Emily recognised it; a place where courting couples strayed to steal a moment's privacy, away from the eyes of interfering busybodies, puzzled as to how the twins had learnt of it.

A deeper voice blended with the treble tones of the twins… a voice the seekers identified instantly, one which also answered Emily's unspoken question.

They looked at each other then back at the folly.

"Lord Stapleton," Emily hissed, under her breath, trying to control her vexation. *What was he thinking? He probably wasn't thinking. For so shrewd a man, he could be remarkably obtuse.*

Their quarry located, Emily and Jenny strolled into the ruin as though naught was amiss.

"Em'ly," Minnie squealed her delight, and skipped across the stone flags to hug Emily's legs, nearly tipping that young lady over. Leaning backwards, the better to look at Emily, she added, "You found us. I *told* Papa 'splorers never get lost."

"We have been looking for Jason's treasure, ready for your story," Matthew interjected importantly.

Masking her agitation — it was not the twins' fault their father was witless — Emily smiled. "Did you find it?"

"No, but this would make a good hiding place."

"'Tis perfect. No one would ever think to look for treasure here," Emily agreed, cheerfully.

Minnie tugged on Emily's cloak, "Are you going to tell us the story now?" Tilting her head in adorable appeal.

Emily crouched until she was eye level with the twins. "Perhaps we ought to save it for another day. You have enjoyed an excellent quest with your father, but if we dally much longer you will miss breakfast, and that will not do."

Seeing their expressions droop, she appeased, "I think there might *just* be a few moments spare for you to take Jenny to feed to ducks." Sending a silent message to Jenny over their heads.

Diverted, the pair all but dragged Jenny out of the ruin and down to the riverbank, talking over each other in childish excitement, blissfully unaware of Emily's agitation. *An adventure with Papa* and *feeding the ducks — what a thrilling morning.*

Chapter Seven

Observing Emily organise his children without so much as a by your leave, an image flitted through Henry's head, gone before he could grasp its meaning.

Dismissing it — and the accompanying sensation his world was slightly off balance — he brushed his coat to remove the dust from the overturned block of stone where he had been sitting.

"Lady Emily." He bowed.

"Don't 'Lady Emily' me, you addlepated, clay-brained, motley minded..." she paused for dramatic effect, "dunderhead."

Henry's face reflected his shock then darkened. "I *beg* your pardon?"

"You are a dunderhead. An addlepated, clay brain—"

Henry lifted a palm. "I heard you the first time."

"Then, why ask me to repeat myself?"

"Because I fail to see why I am suffering the brunt of your vitriol."

"You fail to see..." Emily's voice scaled an octave, and she threw up her hands. "Oh, my Lord. Did it occur to you that the reason your children were wrapped up in coats and boots was because their nursemaid was taking them for their daily promenade? That when she returned from the kitchen with the packet of breadcrumbs, she might panic when it seemed Matthew and Minnie had disappeared into thin, and very cold air?"

"My Lad —"

She stalked across to where he stood and jabbed a gloved finger on his jacket.

"We have spent the last hour combing this bloody park for your children, desperately banking down the increasing dread they had been kidnapped. Jenny deserves a heartfelt apology, and you deserve a swift kick to your thoughtless rear."

With a glare guaranteed to quail a lesser man, Emily flicked an irate hand and turned to stomp out of the belvedere.

She had not taken two steps when a hand snaked around her elbow and jerked her backwards.

"You dare to rebuke me," Henry ground out, secretly impressed with Emily's collection of insults of which a tinker might be proud.

"Who else dare? Not Jenny." Emily retorted scathingly. "She knows better than to question you, but I have no such qualms…"

"Clearly," Henry muttered.

In high dudgeon, Emily carried on as though he had not spoken. "…you cannot throw *me* out onto the street. These are your *children*, not a broadsheet or a cloak, or a…a…"

Tuning out Emily's tirade, Henry found himself captivated by her flashing eyes and heightened colour, the way an errant strand of hair coiled under her chin. Her refusal to be daunted by a man of his status — as her reproof attested — further demonstration of her mettle.

Out of the blue, as he watched her fingers describe indignant arcs to emphasise her grievance, it came to him that to spar with Emily for the rest of his life, would be the greatest gift ever bestowed. *The rest of his life... nonsense. Get a grip man...*

"Henry? Are you listening to me?"

That jolted him from his contemplation. *Wait... she thought of him as Henry? Hmmm... an intriguing notion.*

He heaved a sigh. "Lady Emily, I appreciate you are cross with me, but I meant no harm and would never wish to cause Jenny or any of my staff distress. It was a genuine mistake and, perhaps if you paused in your castigation for one moment, you might hear the apology I have been trying to offer."

Emily opened her mouth to deliver a cutting response, only to have the words die in her throat. Something in Henry's gaze stayed her tongue, and the foreign emotion ruffling the periphery of her consciousness left her breathless and bewildered.

Emily was in a ferment.

In the month since her initial encounter with Lord Stapleton, he had joined the quartet on more than a dozen occasions. Even her impertinent denouncement of his parental capabilities had not dissuaded him, following which, she did not expect to see him ever again... despite that curious moment. She still blushed in recollection of her audacity.

Henry was, it transpired, an amusing companion. He shared humorous anecdotes about his children — making it abundantly clear he was *not* a detached parent, his duties as a marquis, and life in parliament, which Emily found hilarious but did not interest the twins in the slightest. In turn, Emily wove tales from foreign climes, which continued to enthral.

While Matthew and Minnie burnt off their boundless energy, the two adults chatted about this and that, nothing of any real consequence, their attention on the children rather than each other — at least to a casual observer.

Their friendship... if this budding rapport could be described thus, blossomed, but only within the margins of their morning rendezvous. Emily, intent on keeping her counsel regarding the widower she hardly knew, relished the anonymity. To broadcast their... association transformed it into something tangible and she was not ready.

She might never be ready.

That anonymity had just come to a screeching halt in the shape of an invitation from Lord Stapleton asking whether she would be so kind as to be his guest at an upcoming ball.

Hosted by the Duke and Duchess of Droitwich, this was the ball which launched the various Christmas festivities — everyone who was anyone would be there. No one in their right mind would forfeit the opportunity to forget the cold dark of winter, if only for an evening.

To accompany Henry would set tongues gossiping. Conversely, the invitation stated it was a masquerade ball — a cleverly designed mask might provide disguise enough for her to mingle with her peers unrecognised. Oh, but they would be announced... *this was a bad idea.*

Slapping the invitation on her palm, Emily registered how frequently, of late, Henry Bartholomew distracted her. Contorting her pretty face into a fierce grimace, she tried to fathom the reason.

His image appeared before her as though she had conjured him out of the air. Tall, but not too tall. Dark haired with a smattering of grey at his temples. Twinkling eyes, the colour of woodsmoke. *Dear me, girl... woodsmoke indeed... you are waxing lyrical.* She allowed herself a grin and continued her internal appraisal.

He rarely smiled, unless the children were around, but his demeanour was grave rather than remote. That his thoughts might be heavy, gave Emily pause. *Did he dwell on the past? Did he miss his wife? Had they been deliriously happy together?* Studiously ignoring the curious ache *those* notions engendered.

His attire was of the highest quality, but ever-so slightly rumpled, enhancing the erroneous impression he was perpetually pre-occupied. He reminded her of one of Nathaniel's university professors — an incurable scatterbrain about practically everything except his subject — the classics. The moment Professor Wynyard stepped into a classroom, he became razor sharp, and woe betide anyone who tried to outwit him.

Henry was similarly disposed as their recent altercation corroborated. A man not to be underestimated. A man who probably never did anything without evaluating his decision from every angle — probably a whizz at chess.

A man unlikely to invite a lady to a ball on a whim.

Oh my…

. . .

Emily was pacing the parlour no closer to a decision when she heard the front doorbell chime, followed by a muffled conversation.

Moments later, Mr Walters knocked on the door to ask whether she was receiving.

"Lady Juliette," he intoned.

"Oh, what perfect timing. Please show her in." Her relief was palpable. "Juliette," she cried as her sister-in-law entered the room, "just the person. I have a conundrum."

"Gracious, Emily, what has you so rattled?" Juliette Livingston's mouth quirked at Emily's obvious agitation. "You are fairly fizzing."

"I have been invited to a ball," Emily wailed.

"Which is perturbing because…" Juliette drew out the last word.

"With a marquis."

"I might need a soupçon more." Juliette shooed Emily over to the fire and, after they had made themselves comfortable in the aged leather chairs, the latter divulged her quandary. It took some time because Emily's brain and mouth refused to work in harmony and her words tripped over one another.

"Let me get this straight. As a result of two children colliding with you in the park, you met their father, which resulted in this invite?" Juliette clarified.

"Not quite so simplistic but, essentially, yes." Emily chewed at the corner of her bottom lip and eyed Juliette, dubiously.

"I fail to understand your dilemma."

"He is a widower, with two children. I am a spinster who absconded for several years without explanation. Not to mention the incident when I upbraided him with a singular lack of tact."

"You, tactless? Emily Livingston, for shame." Juliette flattened her mouth in an effort to suppress her mirth, her friend's imprudence well-known.

"The crux of the matter being, does not my accompanying him to a ball convey intention?"

Emily's decidedly unenthusiastic tone and disgruntled expression was Juliette's undoing and she dissolved into laughter. "Oh, my dear, do not take on so. 'Tis just a ball. I think you might be reading more into this than is warranted," she paused, and canted her head. "Do you, perchance, like the aforementioned gentleman?"

"Juliette," Emily remonstrated.

"Emily," Juliette mimicked, grinning wickedly.

"Do not tease, and no. I do not think of him in... in... in a..." Emily floundered, "...a romantic sense. I daresay Lord Stapleton is being kind and probably invited me out of a misguided sense of pity."

"Does he strike you as a man who behaves in such a manner?"

Emily rubbed her nose. "No, he does not, so why..." she trailed off.

"Did it ever occur to you that he might harbour an affection for you?"

Now it was Emily's turn to chortle. "For me. Get away with you," using one of Jenny's favourite ripostes. "He's a marquis."

"Which has what to do with anything," Juliette countered with blithe disregard for grammar.

"What reason could he have to court me? While my dowry is not paltry, I am regarded as well past marriageable age, and 'tis unlikely I am of interest to a man of his distinction. Also, have you considered he might still be in love with his wife? A courtship is probably the last thing on his mind."

"Pfft, if that was the case, I doubt he would be taking time out of his busy schedule to meet you on the banks of the

Serpentine in the middle of winter. Christina Bartholomew died... oh, let me think..." Juliette ruminated, "...the twins were babes. I'd say nigh on four years ago. Theirs was an arranged union, although they seemed happy."

Emily's expression told Juliette this was not enough to convince her.

"Even if he loved his wife, that does not mean he cannot love again, and do not demean yourself, Emily. Perhaps he is attracted to you, not Emily the daughter of a marquis but you as a person in your own right. Not every marriage is born of duty or expectation. Your brother and I married for love."

"You are among the fortunate few."

"Hmmm, what of Ged and Melissa?" Juliette named two of their circle, whose fictitious courtship — devised to thwart their respective parents' aspirations — had bloomed into genuine and enduring attraction.

"What of Randolph?" Emily referred to the remaining and very grumpy bachelor of the close-knit trio, completed by Nathaniel and Ged. "Love did not win him fair lady."

Juliette tapped her nose, knowingly. "Until this last week or so, I might have conceded your point, but my instinct tells me his jaded outlook is about to change drastically. No," when Emily looked ready to launch into an interrogation, "I think 'tis better I keep my peace... a little longer."

"Tsk, I cry unfair, but respect your discretion," Emily grumbled, good-naturedly.

Chapter Eight

There was a short silence, then Juliette — as was her habit — jumped in where angels feared to tread. "Why do you reject the notion of love when once you espoused it?"

Startled, Emily stared at the younger woman, not because she was perturbed by Juliette's question, but because she had forgotten about James. She had not thought of him in days, even weeks.

"I cannot see him anymore," she whispered, forlornly.

Juliette reached for Emily's hand and squeezed gently. "'Tis a natural progression, Em. A sign you are moving beyond your sorrow. To cling to something, which has gone will not revive it… or him, however much we crave it to be so," she consoled, "and you cannot dwell in the past. What would James tell you to do?"

Emily flushed. Juliette echoed her father's admonition of three months ago. "I miss him," she confessed, vexed that all her hard work, her determination to move on was obliterated in that one sentence.

"Of course, you do, and he remains in your heart. You will

always hold a part of him, but that part needs to be wrapped in tissue, boxed up, and stored in your memory, not in your future."

"I was certain I had achieved that. Papa and I talked on the way home from your wedding, and I realised I had to say goodbye, I thought I had…"

"Perhaps your absence is what makes it so difficult," Juliette mused.

"How exactly?" Emily frowned in puzzlement.

"When someone dies, everything around you triggers reminders. Places, people, food, particular gowns, sunlight, moonlight, dogs, horses… everything… even the rain. You left shortly after learning of his death. When you returned, you had to experience all those things as though they were fresh, not part of your past, and it must seem as though it happened mere days ago not four years. You are not betraying James by attending a ball with another gentleman."

"When did you get to be so wise?" Emily summoned up a cheeky smile, to lighten an atmosphere grown solemn.

"It comes from being an old married woman," Juliette, the newlywed, contended facetiously, fluttering an imperious hand.

"I declare you will never be an old married woman, not even in your dotage." Emily's giggle was infectious and the room resounded with their merriment.

"Now," Juliette redirected their conversation, as Mr Walters came in bearing a tray of refreshments, "about this ball."

"At least 'tis a masquerade ball, mayhap no one will recognise me."

"We have been invited also, so, you will be surrounded by friends," Juliette coaxed.

"You believe I should accept?"

"Absolutely."

Four nights hence, promptly at eight, Henry rapped on the door of Deerhurst Lodge. He tried not to fidget while he waited, quashing an overwhelming urge to run, and made do with yanking at his cravat which he swore was choking him. *This was madness, what was he thinking?*

Too late, a white-haired, smartly liveried man opened the door and granted him entry.

Henry stepped inside and was rendered momentarily speechless.

Straight ahead, he saw Emily descending the stairs. She looked… unreal — a figment of his imagination.

Her gown, of the richest turquoise, was overlaid with exquisite lace, the deeper hue catching the candlelight as she moved. Her hair was caught up in an intricate bun, shining curls framing her anxious face.

In one hand, she held her reticule, a fan, and a silvery blue mask. Behind her, a maid carried a long cloak in midnight blue, trimmed with cream fur. Emily stopped on the bottom stair, and the maid draped the warm material around her shoulders.

"My lady," Henry's tone was reverent as he swept a chival-rous bow.

Emily dipped a curtsy, glad he could not see how her legs trembled. "My lord."

"Shall we?" He crooked his elbow, pleased when she slid her hand around his arm, her fingers coming to rest lightly on his sleeve.

The maid, whom Emily introduced as Tess, followed them out of the house. Despite Emily assuring her father she had no need of a chaperone, the marquis disagreed.

"I trust Lord Stapleton to be a man above reproach, but you are my daughter and, until you are wed, remain my responsibility whether you are twenty and one or sixty and one, and that is my last word," he had stated emphatically.

This is not to say Emily's acquiescence was gracious, there was much grousing and harrumphing but, in the end, acknowledging her father would win, yielded to the inevitable — albeit grudgingly.

The unshuttered windows of the Duke and Duchess of Droitwich's palatial residence were illuminated by the count-less candelabra within.

Carriage after carriage drew up, horses stamping their feet and tossing silky manes in the chill night air.

Exquisitely attired passengers alighted, ascending the broad sweep of steps, to be greeted by a uniformed footman at the great front doors which stood open in welcome.

The ball was in full swing when Emily and Henry arrived. Doffing her cloak in the retiring room, assuring Tess she was not at risk of being compromised, and making sure her mask was in place, Emily found Henry, and the couple joined the queue of guests.

Glad of the mask when they were announced, Emily heaved a sigh of relief when when no one seemed in the slightest interested in the lady on the Marquis of Stapleton's arm.

Blissfully unaware of Emily's diffidence, Henry ushered her to a table at the far end of the dance floor where Juliette and Nathaniel, along with Melissa and Ged, were sitting.

As the two men stood, Emily spotted her twin assessing

Henry obliquely... which, it must be said, did *not* go unnoticed by the latter.

When Nate drew her into a quick hug, she murmured in his ear, "Please do not feel obliged to interfere. I am perfectly capable of looking after myself."

Nathaniel jerked back to search his sister's face. "Em..."

"I know you worry, and I love you for it, but I am not a child anymore."

Nathaniel held her gaze. "No, I keep forgetting that. Just... please be careful."

"When am I not?" She winked.

Juliette, aware Nathaniel tended to be over-protective of his only sister and twin to boot, grasped his hand. "I do believe 'tis time we danced."

"I apologise for my brother," Emily opened her palms in a placatory fashion as Nathaniel whisked his wife away. "He..."

"He is doing what every brother ought. You have no reason to apologise. I would be disheartened if he showed no concern." Henry smiled. "Now, let us enjoy the evening. Please do me the honour of this dance?"

Suddenly, Emily relaxed, and allowed Henry to escort her onto the dance floor. The glittering ballroom was a kaleidoscope of light and colour, music and chatter. Polished surfaces and gilt edged mirrors glistened under the flicker of candles. Exotic-looking vines trailed around graceful columns, and vases overflowing with fragrant blooms created the illusion of a warm summer's day.

As was often the case at the first significant event of any Season, but more pronounced at this time of the year, the atmosphere was one akin to giddy relief. The dazzling opulence in striking contrast with the long dark of winter and, for a while, they could lose themselves in the magic.

Emily and Henry danced a set, then returned to their table, immediately becoming embroiled in a nonsensical discussion with their four friends.

At some stage during the evening, Juliette nudged Emily and, surreptitiously, wagged her fan towards a couple on the dance floor.

"I told you so." She grinned impishly. "By the time the night is over, Randolph will have declared his hand."

Emily observed the tall earl, who was gazing down at his partner as though he was holding the wealth of the world when all he expected was a penny.

"With whom is he dancing?" she quizzed, aware of a vague ache which she dispatched as whimsy.

"Emma Newbury, daughter of the Viscount Aspley." Juliette's tone was nothing short of smug.

"Was he not the gentleman who died under a cloud regarding shady business dealings?"

"The very same, although I do not think I am breaching any confidences when I say the cloud is about to be lifted. Major Withers and some of his team have been working to clear the unfortunate man's name. Not that it is of much use to him, but I'm sure it will gladden the hearts of his family."

"Poor Emma," Emily murmured, conscious of how quickly fortunes could change. "I trust Randolph will not cause her any more sorrow."

"I suspect Nathaniel and Ged will drop him down a well if he does." Juliette chuckled, glancing at the two men in question.

"Without a second thought," Ged affirmed, his face alight with humour.

His comment relegated Randolph and Emma to the background, for the time being, and the conversation around the table moved onto other topics.

53

Chapter Nine

As the clock crept closer to midnight, Henry — who had been gratifyingly attentive — removed his mask and excused himself, saying he would return forthwith.

Absently, Emily watched him go, admiring his upright bearing as he strode across the room, waylaid now and again by people he knew.

An elderly man greeted him, and the two exchanged a few words, during which the former introduced a beautiful young lady, who simpered as Henry bowed politely. A brief conversation ensued, then Henry inclined his head and continued on through the huge glass doors.

No more than a heartbeat later, the young lady hurried after him. To Emily's consternation, she felt her chest tighten, jarred by an unfamiliar stab of jealousy.

Stop it, she chided internally. *You have no claim on Henry. He is naught but a... a... friend...* not entirely sure what their relationship was anymore.

She glowered at the doors as a series of completely different scenes unfolded in her mind's eye. Walking the empty paths of Hyde Park with Henry, so close, they almost touched. Their banter, amiable debates, and fleeting disagreements. His rare smile, his beautiful hands, his mesmerising gaze.

That same peculiar prickle, Emily had discerned all those weeks ago assailed her. A prickle, if she was true to herself, happened whenever she thought about him.

Was it remotely possible? No... he had two children to consider. The twins... the notion another might supplant her in the twins' affections was as painful as losing Henry. *Losing Henry? She didn't* have *him to lose. Oh, this was such a mess.*

"Bless my soul, Emily, you look fierce enough to intimidate the devil himself. What has confounded you so badly?" Melissa's quiet question penetrated the uproar in Emily's head.

"Henry Bartholomew," Juliette opined, slyly.

"So, that is the way the wind blows," empathy warmed Melissa's remark.

"No, 'tis not, only, but now..." Emily hesitated, fiery colour staining her cheeks. She clapped cool fingers to her face. "Oh my."

"I wondered when you were going to realise." Juliette shook her head in amusement. "I alluded to this very thing the other day, and recall you were vehemently opposed to my intimation."

"Ahhh... mayhap a case of the lady doth protest too much?" Melissa asked.

"I cannot be," Emily groaned. "'Tis ludicrous."

"Why?" this from Juliette.

"Well... because him... and the children... and his wife..."

"Em, you are not making any sense," Melissa interrupted Emily's babble.

"I know, I need a moment." Emily stood so abruptly her chair fell over, the sudden clatter drawing the astonished glances of several guests. Her flaming cheeks turning puce, she righted it and fled.

Emily's impetuous dash was arrested when she reached a pair of velvet curtains in rich cerise, drawn back to reveal an open door leading to a balcony.

A cool breeze enticed her to step through. Slipping off her mask, she peered around the heavy material, unwilling to disturb a couple sharing an intimate moment — exhaling a relieved sigh to see she was alone.

She scarcely noticed the hardy winter roses, flowering tenaciously under the balcony; their delicate pink hues warming the grey of the marble columns.

Slumping onto the stone cap of the elegant balustrade, she strove to untangle the pandemonium swirling in her mind, to no avail. Whichever way she looked at it, and however farfetched it seemed, the answer was staring her in the face... had been all along.

She was irrevocably in love with Henry Bartholomew.

Well, this was a pretty pickle.

The clouds parted and, for a heartbeat, the pale gleam of a moonbeam illuminated her left hand.

James?

"James, if you can hear me, send me a sign so I know you approve, that I am not breaking our oath by giving my heart to another. If, in fact, he wants my heart." *Hark at me. I'm talking to my dead love about a new love... 'tis a good job I am alone.*

Balancing a platter of tasty morsels and two tall glasses of hot chocolate, Henry was distracted by a commotion at the far side of the ballroom, mystified to see Emily disappearing with unladylike haste.

"Has someone upset Lady Emily?" he grilled as he approached their group, placing the tray on a convenient side table.

"Not so much upset, as... hmmm... provoked," Juliette's face was alive with mischief.

"Encouraged, mayhap," Melissa supplied contemplatively.

"Perhaps galvanised..." Juliette's nose wrinkled in thought.

"Wait... more like... awakened," her friend offered.

"*Awakened!* Yes, that is the perfect description." Juliette nodded exultantly.

They looked at Henry and chorused, "Awakened."

Baffled, Henry raked a hand through his short hair. "Please help a man out here. Have I done something to cause her distress?"

"In a manner of speaking," Juliette replied puckishly.

"I must find her."

He spun on his heel, to pivot back around at Juliette's, "Before you pursue your damsel, my lord, ask yourself whether 'tis in simple concern for her well-being, or because knowing you may be the source of her confusion cuts far deeper."

Henry swallowed a sharp retort as he registered both women were eying him expectantly.

"What am I missing here?"

"I think you already know but have yet to acknowledge it." Melissa said. "My... our... only plea is that you do not follow Emily unless your reason is the forever kind."

Her words caught him off guard. "You think my..." he

stopped, a grin beginning to form. "Thank you." He bowed and was gone.

Juliette and Melissa settled into their seats.

"Two in one night... mayhap we should take up match-making." Juliette observed pertly, spying Nathaniel rolling his eyes. "Oh hush. Here." Handing Melissa one of the hot chocolates, taking the other for herself. "No sense in letting these go to waste." She took a sip. "Hmmm... heavenly."

Henry's boots made no sound on the plush rugs as he trod the halls in search of Emily, finally tracking her to the secluded balcony. She was leaning against one of the pillars, looking out into the moonlit garden.

A candelabra, balanced precariously on the balustrade, indicated the hosts anticipated their guests might use this quiet corner, the flickering flames throwing intricate shadows over the cool marble.

He glanced up. Suspended from the ceiling, a mistletoe ball. *Was that a sign? The moon and mistletoe...* for a man not prone to flights of fancy, the coincidence resonated with him.

Once, a lifetime ago, as darkness fell on a corpse-strewn battlefield, Henry was striving to keep a dying man alive until the stretcher bearers or the doctor squelched their way across the acres of sludge and bodies. The soldier's wound was catastrophic, his survival required a miracle which were few and far between.

"Stay with me," Henry had coaxed. "See the moon is rising, and the doctor is coming. Soon you will be in a warm bed, drinking brandy, and all this will be naught but a bad dream."

Brilliant blue eyes, stark in a dirt-smeared, ashen face, had fluttered open. "You are addled," the soldier rasped with a wry grimace, "but I thank you for your optimism," he paused, "and for not leaving me to die alone." His strength failing, he gazed up at the crystal-clear sky where there were no wars, or death, or filthy mounds of mud.

The soft radiance of the moon obscured the horrors surrounding them. A pale beam illuminated the pair, creating the impression they were carved from alabaster — a moment in time caught forever.

Heaving an exhausted sigh, a sound which seemed to encapsulate the futility of their circumstances, the wounded man had grasped Henry's arm, then pointed skywards. "Never forget that if we belong to a universe where moon-beams and mistletoe exist, nothing is insurmountable, for otherwise, what it the point?"

Given where they were, Henry had raised a sceptical brow at such naiveté, but, with a slight shrug, the man smiled wearily. "Against the odds, we prevailed," as his eyes drifted closed for the last time.

Nothing is insurmountable…

Henry prayed it was so.

His impatience to proclaim his affection, to conquer the dread Emily might yet reject him, warred with the, some-what ungallant, urge to study her covertly.

Her brow was creased, suggesting an internal discourse. Her gown shimmered in the glow of the candles giving it a mercurial hue, and he itched to thread his fingers through her lustrous hair, unravelling its dark length, letting it spill in riotous abandon over her shoulders.

Henry had loved his wife... or thought he had. Now he was not so sure. The emotion he felt for Emily bore no resemblance to the placid devotion Christina and he had shared. A marriage arranged from the cradle, the two grew up together, aware their future was already mapped out, and he believed they had been as content as most couples in comparable circumstances.

Then came Emily.

She never strayed far from his thoughts, not even in slumber. A woman of disarming contradictions — at once shy yet vivacious, candid yet reserved, who had no qualms arguing black was white, and red a completely different colour, simply to provoke a response. A courageous, free spirit, who did not apologise for behaviour some might consider... eccentric. A woman who had revelled in challenges, at which men might balk.

These qualities were beguiling, but the defining one... in his humble opinion... was that Emily treated Jenny, a maid, with the same ingenuous friendliness, respect, and dignity as she did his children, as she afforded him and would, undoubtedly, accord every other member of society — regardless of status.

Emily was, in every way, the exception to an unspoken rule.

For a man whose entire existence had adhered to strict guidelines, to succumb to the chaos was intoxicating.

Neither had uttered a single word of affection, yet it sizzled between them. Their conversations, although interesting, rarely delved into the personal, but to Henry it was as though he knew Emily at an elemental level, every facet, every thought, every dream, and every desire.

Their encounters were not frequent, but, of late, he found himself counting the hours until next they met, only then did the inexplicable melancholy, diminish.

A line from Shakespeare flitted through his mind... *parting is such sweet sorrow...*

It was time.

"My lady..."

Chapter Ten

E mily jumped and whirled around at the deep timber of his voice, managing to smother an indecorous squawk. "My Lord," she sketched a curtsey, eying him warily.

"Lady Emily…"

"Oh, do please call me Emily," she beseeched. "We are alone on a balcony. I propose we allow etiquette to take a holiday… if only for this… errr… interlude."

Henry took a step forward, then stopped. Separated by less than a foot, suddenly, crossing the Thames in a single leap seemed easier.

"Am I the reason you sought a quiet corner?" he asked after a moment's silence broken only by the soughing of the breeze through the trees, and the distant strains of music.

"The ballroom was hot. I needed some air." Emily turned away, unwilling to admit anything until she had recovered from the shock of her own epiphany.

"Prevaricating…" he dared tease.

Needled, she spun back. "Why did you follow me?"

"Because we are on the cusp of something extraordinary.

Something, I believe, we ought to explore, discover, expose. Something unexpected, yet infinitely precious. Perhaps my intuition deceives me but, if we do not take a risk, I am convinced we will regret it for the rest of our lives.

"La… Emily, the sensations rampaging through me are unparalleled. We remain little more than strangers, yet with you it is as though I have come home. When you are close, it is all I can do not to entwine our fingers, to enfold you in my arms, to kiss you until you forget everything except we two. My heart misses a beat when you smile. My body aches for you. When we part, the daylight seems to dim.

"I loved Christina." Henry saw Emily flinch, but persevered. Without honesty, without trust, there was nothing, and a new love could not flourish while a ghost of the old still lurked. "Ours was an unruffled love, sweet and comfortable and, until I met you, I never questioned the sentiment.

"The emotions you stir in me cannot be labelled. They are wild, untamed, raw, and volatile, yet they are also tender, sensuous, bewitching, and unquenchable.

"I disregarded them at first, presuming they were driven by lust. A lonely widower meets a beautiful young lady whose joie de vivre is a tangible thing — a titillating tale more suited to the gossip columns — which, while devilishly attractive, could not endure… could it…? Surely, it was nothing more than a flight of fancy.

"As days became weeks, to deny what my heart insisted was love, to pretend it was fleeting, that it would melt with the winter's snow was to deny my very soul. My greatest desire is that your regard might extend beyond me being the father of the two scamps who literally barged into your life.

"Emily, in a handspan of time you have become my everything. I know 'tis too soon, and this confession may be precipitous, but when I envisage my life without you, it is a colourless void. I love you with every fibre of my being and, should you be amenable to my suit, I swear on everything I hold dear that whatever life the good Lord grants me will be devoted to your happiness."

He took a breath, the soldier's benediction echoing in his mind.

"Here we are bathed in moonlight and standing under a mistletoe ball. I have heard it said that if we belong to a universe where moonbeams and mistletoe exist, nothing is insurmountable, for otherwise, what is the point? A quixotic notion perhaps, but when it comes to love, there should be no ambiguity."

He stopped, his heart thudding with the intensity of his feelings, desperate for Emily to understand this was no frivolous dalliance in a quiet corner at a masked ball.

This was forever.

Stunned, Emily gaped at Henry. His earnest declaration was reminiscent of her favourite fairy tales, of myths and legends, but this was no fantasy.

Never mind that, where had he heard those words? James' words.
She had pleaded for a sign...
None could be as incontrovertible.

"Henry..." her breath held in too long, whooshed out of her lungs, making her cough.

In an instant he was by her side to stroke her back in a soothing motion... *decorum be damned*. When she attempted to pull away, he did not relinquish his embrace and she felt the brush of his lips on her hair.

"H-Henry..." she stammered.

He pulled back slightly, and their eyes met. "Yes?" His

guarded grey gaze reflected the candlelight, laying bare a vulnerability she had not noticed before.

It warmed her that in this they were equals. Grappling with a swath of emotions which, if misinterpreted, could undermine as easily as they could empower.

"Henry…" *Come on, woman. He knows his name.* "I confess, I am similarly inclined." She nearly giggled when his eyebrows shot under his rakish forelock. *Hmm, it* was *rakish, how had this escaped her attention? Because you tend to focus on his smoky eyes and kissable lips… Emily concentrate…*

"Sorry, where was I… oh yes… I too once believed I knew what true love was, and his death was the spur for my unorthodox expedition."

Henry's arms tightened a fraction, but he did not speak.

"He was killed in the final weeks of the wars, during the last gasp of a madman determined to regain what would never be surrendered. I was angry, distraught, and mired in a grief so deep I did not think I would ever recover.

"So, I ran away, as far as I could go where nothing reminded me of him, of us. It was four years before I found the courage to set foot on English soil again.

"My grand plan was to remain a spinster, to be a wonderful aunt to my nieces and nephews without risking my heart. Then Fate saw fit to meddle, using your children as her snare — she is a crafty wench — and my complacency was tossed out with the bathwater.

"Your children… Henry, your children…."

She flung herself out of his grasp, flailing her hands erratically, muttering about upsetting the twins and evil stepmothers.

Henry bit his lip at her wild gesticulations. "Emily, sweetheart, the twins love you as much as I do… well perhaps not *quite* as much." His mock salacious grin drawing a reluctant chuckle from Emily. "Time enough to apprise them if necessary. You were saying?"

Emily registered the reticence in Henry's voice. He thought she might reject his petition. A wicked thrill rippled through her and, before her head talked her out of it, she kissed him full on the lips.

She heard his sharp intake of breath, followed by a juddering sigh as he reciprocated with sinfully, seductive mastery.

"Yes," she murmured when, eventually, they broke for air. "Yes, I love you. Yes, I am amenable to your suit, and I swear on everything I hold dear that whatever life the good Lord grants me will be devoted to showing you how much you mean to me."

Which, of course, earned her another ardent kiss; something, Emily decided as she descended into a dizzy spiral, she was going to like...*a lot*!

"Henry," Emily asked a *long* time later. "Where did you hear that phrase, the one about moonbeams and mistletoe?"

"'Tis not a tale for lady's ears."

"I think you will find I am not easily distraught. Please." She squeezed his fingers, feeling the light pressure when he returned the gesture.

Henry was quiet for so long, Emily expected a rebuff. Cupping his cheek, she repeated, "Please. Oh," another thought struck her, "unless the telling will be too distressing."

"Time and distance cushion the anguish, but war is a savage business. Are you sure?"

She kissed his knuckles and held their clasped hands against her heart. "Yes."

He paused, corralling his thoughts.

"It was late afternoon, dusk was already fading to night but several of us continued to scour the battlefield for survivors who..." he paused, trying to think of the least disturbing description "...were unable to get back to camp. It was slow going because it was easy to miss a comrade in the gloom.

"I came across a soldier who had suffered a grievous wound. A man I did not recognise, in itself not unusual, given the different regiments. I tried to stem the bleeding, to alleviate his pain, but I was unable to help him." Henry's voice took on a faraway note. "No one had anything with which to help him.

"I tried to make him comfortable, held him, kept him warm, talked to him, but he was slipping away and there was nothing I could do. I had seen men fall to a bullet, or cannon fire but, until that moment, had never watched as my fellow man passed from this life to the next. I felt utterly powerless.

"I could hear the auxiliaries approaching, I begged him to fight, even knowing my plea was futile. He came back to full consciousness, looked up at the sky, and uttered those words. I thought him naive, but he was adamant. He died before the stretcher bearers reached us.

"He is buried among his comrades. His name was James..."

"Vernon," Emily whispered through dry lips.

"How on earth do you know..." Henry stopped as it dawned on him. "Oh, my dearest darling."

"I asked for a sign." Emily could not prevent a sob. "I asked for a sign, he approved of you, that he had released me from my vow. You... and moonbeams and..." she burst into a storm of weeping.

Safe in Henry's arms, the tears she had held at bay for

nearly five years spilled out like a waterfall after the winter's thaw.

"Good gracious, I am a veritable watering pot. How discourteous, especially after your beautiful proposal." She smiled tremulously, dabbing at her eyes with the snowy white handkerchief Henry had thoughtfully pressed into her hand, regaining her composure.

Henry brushed his lips to hers. "If I cannot provide a shoulder for a few tears, I would prove a woeful husband, and if not for James..." he had no need to elaborate, his grey eyes tender.

"And 'tis a wonderful shoulder," Emily murmured snuggling against him. "Oh, you are thoroughly irresistible. I am astounded it took me so long to realise."

"Irresistible... hmmm... I can see we are going to agree on most everything," Henry quipped. "Hey," when Emily elbowed him. "That's no way to treat your beloved betrothed."

"Beloved betrothed? So, 'tis official?"

"You said yes." He grazed the tip of his nose along hers, sending delicious tingles all the way to Emily's toes. "A verbal agreement is binding. To recant would be deemed unladylike..."

"I have never fancied myself to be ladylike, but perhaps, just this once..." Emily interposed dreamily, hypnotised by his eyes.

"...and would break my heart..." his voice lowered to a growl.

"Well, that would never do." Their lips hovered tantalisingly close.

A sudden draft caught the curtains, the candles guttered, and shaft of moonlight fell on the couple.

"Moonbeams and mistletoe," Henry murmured against her mouth. "'Tis true, what else do we need?"

"I need you to kiss me." Emily blushed, unaccountably shy.

He did.

Epilogue

Winter 1821

Bundled up in far too many blankets, Emily Bartholomew, Marchioness of Stapleton was relaxing in an old rocking chair — one she had unearthed in the attics, shortly after her wedding, deciding it deserved a second chance. Repaired, re-cushioned, and polished, it looked like new and was distinctly more commodious than the contemporary models.

A wintry breeze wafted through the window — which Emily had demanded be opened, overruling vociferous opposition — carrying with it the faintest hint of pine.

Supremely content and, it must be admitted, a trifle complacent, Emily studied the sleeping faces of the two infants nestled in her arms as she rocked back and forth gently.

"My darling, you must be exhausted, you should rest," Henry Bartholomew implored, witness to the agonies his wife had suffered over the previous however many hours.

"I am not tired, my love. Well, mayhap a little," she

conceded at Henry's disbelieving brow, "but I cannot let them go. I fear if I put them in the cradle when I awake it will be naught but a dream. Look at what we created." Her awed tones pulling a grin from her husband.

"*We*? I cannot claim much credit, you did all the hard work."

"Yet without you, we would not have these precious poppets, and the... errr... preparatory measures were sublime." Her chaste words at odds with her saucy smile.

"Minx." Henry's grin morphed into a quiet chuckle, and he kissed her forehead.

About to reply, she was overtaken by a prodigious yawn. "I am sorry, how impolite."

"Em, you have nothing to apologise for, but humour a poor husband and let me help you back to bed, even if only for an hour."

He relieved her of the drowsy infants, one by one, and tucked them into the double cradle. He stared down at the pair as they wriggled, tiny fists bunched, then settled into a deeper slumber. "Twins..." he shook his head. "I am still confounded."

Emily's eyes brimmed with mirth. Henry's shock when the doctor announced he could hear two heartbeats, had not dissipated. "And I still fail to see how, given both our families are littered with twins, and 'tis not as though we had any say in the matter."

As though carrying a fragile piece of the finest china, Henry assisted Emily to their bed, arranging the pillows and covers until she was comfortable.

She grasped Henry's hand. "Matthew and Minnie," she slurred, eyelids drooping.

"I shall bring them home later. I am uncertain I shall ever be able to pry them from Juliette's clutches, she seems loath to part with them." Henry could not fathom why anyone would want to *extend* time with his rambunctious seven-year-old duo.

"She is practicing." Emily yawned again and, before Henry could extract further details, had fallen fast asleep.

Henry's amusement at his wife's vagary, ebbed as he studied her.

The foreboding he might lose Emily during childbirth persisted, and he was determined she would not throw herself back into her daily routine immediately, despite her insistence that lying a-bed was detrimental.

"While on my travels, I talked with women from diverse cultures, and was interested to learn that most are up and about within hours of the birth, gradually becoming more active. They believe it aids recovery because the body stays limber, and the blood does not grow sluggish." she had said during one of their *many* discussions on the subject.

"I know you want to cosset me, and I love you for it, but I believe a protracted confinement will do more harm than good. I promise to rest when I am tired and will not overdo it, but I prefer not to stagnate in bed for weeks. If, for no other reason than the boredom will drive me to insanity, and Beldam is not ready for me." Kissing him by way of delicious distraction.

To argue was a waste of breath. His worry did not abate, he simply kept it to himself.

He watched until Emily's breathing evened out, dropped a light kiss on her cheek, slid his hand out of her clasp, and crept from the room, leaving her under the protective eye of Jenny.

Henry had refused to countenance a long betrothal, and the couple were married with appropriate pomp and celebration four months after their first meeting.

Breaking with tradition, the ceremony was held by the Serpentine, at night — to the resigned astonishment of their friends and family who declared them unhinged.

To be fair, when Henry floated his idea, Emily — while enchanted — did feel moved to remark that the arrangement was somewhat impractical.

Henry was not to be swayed. "We met on the banks of Serpentine, and avowed our love under the moon. Trust me, I have everything in hand."

Poetic may have been his reasoning but Henry, as good as his word, organised everything. He rallied a small army of friends and, together, they transformed the old belvedere into something straight out of a fairy tale.

Candelabra adorned every ledge, lamps hung from tree branches. He had even appropriated, although no one knew from where, an enormous rug which covered the cold flag-stones, protecting feet in delicate footwear.

The pièce de résistance was the mistletoe ball, Henry had procured, then suspended from an overhanging bough. This final decorative element flummoxed their guests, especially as it was several weeks after Christmas, but the couple in question, sharing a secret smile, maintained an enigmatic silence. Some things were best left unsaid.

Telling the twins had gone more smoothly than Emily anticipated. Despite Henry's assurances to the contrary, she harboured a vague unease about their reaction, and took pains to remind him of the various wicked stepmothers which appeared in the folk tales and myths they read with avidity.

"What if they think I am usurping them in your affection?" she had brooded.

"Emily, they adore you. I cannot imagine they will think any such thing, and we will not know until we talk to them," had been Henry's philosophical response.

As Henry predicted, Matthew and Minnie's whoops of joy obliterated Emily's qualms.

When, eventually, the pair calmed down and stopped bouncing around the room, Minnie, head cocked on one side, had asked, "You will be our mama?"

Emily had glanced at Henry who inclined his head with a heart-melting smile. She nodded slowly. "Yes... as lo—"

She got no further. With an ecstatic shriek, Minnie flung her arms around Emily's neck and scattered kisses over her face. "We love you, Em'ly. See," over her shoulder she had informed Matthew, haughtily, "I *told* you we get to play with Em'ly foooorevaah."

"Forever and a day, and I love you two too." Emily had reciprocated in kind, then tickled the child until she chortled with glee.

"Minnie, it's M a m a. Not Emily," Matthew, the ever-corrective brother, tutted before abandoning his dignity to join the tangle of arms and legs.

Their antics at the wedding, had stolen the evening!

Winter 1822

Christmas Eve: the house, festooned from top to bottom with holly, ivy, laurel, and pine, interspersed with paper decorations painstakingly cut out by Matthew and Minnie was quiet.

Four small children — two of whom were wildly excited about the morrow, two of whom had no idea what the fuss was about — were finally in bed.

"Peace at last," Emily sank into the comfortable sofa by the roaring fire in their bedchamber and accepted a glass of port from her husband. "Thank you, my love, I need this." She took a large sip. "Ahhh… that is nectar."

Henry chuckled. "I did not think those rascals would ever go to sleep. How many stories?"

"Five, or maybe six, I lost count." Emily grinned. "I suspect Matthew and Minnie were feigning slumber but am happy to leave them to Jenny's tender mercies for once. I am only thankful Xander and Selene are still too young to participate in their mischief."

One-year-old, Alexander Bartholomew, along with his twin, Selene were, currently, merely spectators to their older siblings' capers — a respite their doting parents knew was fleeting.

Choosing names for their younger twins had sparked lengthy discussions, in the days after their birth — a debate no one was winning. The mites were nearly two weeks old when Minnie begged them to call her baby sister Aphrodite.

"While I do love that name," Emily, fighting to keep a straight face, had mustered up every ounce of diplomacy she possessed — no mean feat, "perhaps something a little less… errr… flamboyant. She is just a wee babe. Wait, maybe…" she had a brainwave, "…will you help me?"

Minnie, feeling very important, agreed and the pair pored over books on myths and legends, pondering some names and discounting others until they came across Selene — Greek goddess of the moon. This gained instant approval from Minnie, unaware of the sentimental meaning the name bore for her parents.

Matthew, enamoured of military heroes from the ancient world, clamoured for his brother to be named for Alexander the Great. All agreed, his choice was the perfect fit.

Minnie, with typical insouciance shortened it to Xander because, as she explained, gravely, Alexander needed too many tongues — so, Selene and Xander they became.

"Aye, enjoy it while it lasts." Henry walked across to the mantlepiece to get his pipe. "They'll catch up soon enough."

"In the twinkling of an eye. They are growing so fast." She blew a sigh.

"You sound a tad weary, perhaps an early night?" Henry recommended. "The children run you ragged."

Emily studied him in the firelight. The flames leaping in the hearth, accentuated his craggy features.

She was endlessly amazed by the sheer depth of love she bore for this quiet, unassuming man. A love beyond reason or explanation. A love which grew stronger every day. A love she knew was returned one-hundredfold.

She thought their life, their family was complete. Four

children, each one a treasure more precious than the costliest gem.

"Henry…" she sounded uncharacteristically hesitant.

Concentrating on lighting his pipe, Henry murmured a preoccupied, "Hmmm."

"I have some news to impart and 'tis best you take a seat."

Henry glanced across the room. About to make a wise-crack about Emily's solemnity, something in his wife's expression stayed his sally. "What is it, Em?"

She patted the sofa. "Sit with me."

"With pleasure." He grinned and did as she bade, gathering her close and kissing her forehead.

Momentarily, Emily relaxed into his arms then straightened up. "My fatigue is not solely related to chasing after our children." She looked down twiddling with her gown, folding and unfolding the material, until it resembled an old dishrag.

Henry grasped her fingers, brushed his lips to her knuckles then searched her face. "Em…?"

"I'm increasing," she whispered, holding his gaze, apprehension radiating off her.

"You are expecting a babe? When? How?"

She nodded. "Doctor Addison says I am about four months gone. As for the how…" She slid her hand under his waistcoat and under his shirt, hearing him suck in a breath as her cool fingers tiptoed over his warm skin. "…do I have to spell it out?" Her wicked smile broke through her anxiety.

"You are a wanton hussy," Henry kissed her soundly.

"I know," she gasped when they came up for air. "Is it not divine?"

"Yes, but don't change the subject. Why did you not tell me sooner?"

"I wanted to be sure, and also…" she paused, "we already have four children, and it might be twins," she finished mournfully.

Henry could not contain a chuckle.

"I am glad you find this funny," she grumbled. "*You* do not have to give birth."

"I wish I could relieve you of this burden, regrettably that is beyond my power. What *is* in my power is ensuring your every need and comfort is met."

"I know, but…"

Standing, Henry drew his wife upright, led her to the French doors which opened onto their private balcony, and heedless of the chill night air, ushered her outside. Enfolding Emily in his arms, her back to his chest, he pointed to the ball of greenery hanging above them, then swung his hand skywards.

The moon and her celestial guardians twinkled down, suffusing the couple in ethereal luminescence.

"See… in a universe where moonbeams and mistletoe exist, nothing is insurmountable."

"You old softy." She turned in his arms to bestow a tender kiss, which quickly became heated, and, for a while, everything else faded away as they surrendered to their ardour.

Turned out… he was right!

About the Author

Rosie Chapel lives in Perth, Australia with her hubby and three furkids. When not writing, she loves catching up with friends, burying herself in a book (or three), discovering the wonders of Western Australia, or — and the best — a quiet evening at home with her husband, enjoying a glass of wine and a movie.

Website: www.rosiechapel.com

Other Books by Rosie Chapel

The Daffodil Garden

The Unconventional Duchess

Rescuing Her Knight

Elusive Hearts - *An Unexpected Romance*: Book One

His Fiery Hoyden

A Regency Duet

A Regency Christmas Double

Fate is Curious

A Christmas Prayer *with Ashlee Shades*

The Lady's Wager - *Surrendered Hearts*: Book Two

Winning Emma - *Surrendered Hearts*: Book Three

A Love Impossible

Unravelling Roana

Love Kindled

Fairy Tale Romance

Chasing Bluebells

Contemporary Romances

Of Ruins and Romance

All At Once It's You

Cobweb Dreams

Just One Step

His Heart's Second Sigh

Dystopian Romance

Echoes & Illusions *with Rori Bleu*

Historical Fiction/Romance

The Pomegranate Tree

Hannah's Heirloom - Book One

Hoping to trace the origins of an ancient ruby clasp, a gift from her long dead grandmother, Hannah Wilson travels to the fortress of Masada with her best friend, Max. Strange dreams concerning a rebel ambush begin to haunt Hannah and following a tragic accident, she slips into the world of Ancient Masada.

A woman out of time, Hannah must rely on her instincts and her knowledge of what will befall this citadel to survive. Will she escape, or is she doomed to die along with hundreds of others as Masada falls — and what does any of this have to do with an ancient ruby clasp?

Echoes of Stone and Fire

Hannah's Heirloom - Book Two

Pompeii - a vibrant city lost in time following the AD79 eruption of Vesuvius. Now rediscovered, archaeologists yearn for an opportunity to uncover the town's past. Some things, however, are best left alone - revealing the secrets hidden beneath the stones could prove perilous. Hannah and Max are brought to Pompeii by a surprise invitation to join an excavation team who are trying to uncover the city's long history.

After entering an excavated house that bears a Hebrew inscription, Hannah's two worlds collide, and she falls back through time to ancient Pompeii. A place where her ancestor is a physician to gladiators engaged in mortal combat, where riotous mobs run amok and where a ghost from the past returns to haunt her.

Will Hannah and her loved ones manage to escape the devastation she knows is coming, before the town is engulfed in volcanic ash? Will she ever find her way back to Max the love of her life, waiting not so patiently millennia away? Or will echoes be all that remain?

Embers of Destiny

Hannah's Heirloom - Book Three

AD80 - Hannah and Maxentius must embark on a new journey to Northern Britannia. This harsh frontier is far from the comforts of Rome and danger lurks where least expected; a garrison of soldiers, some unhappy with their isolated posting; local tribes, outwardly accepting of their Roman occupier, but who may still resent the seizure of their lands.

Millennia away, Hannah Vallier finds a familiar item while working in a museum near Hadrian's Wall. It is the pomegranate; carved by Maxentius on Masada. Before Hannah can discuss it with Max, disaster strikes! Believing her husband has been killed, Hannah retreats into the past, her soul melding with that of her ancestor, but with little idea of what they could face. Is the risk from the conquered tribes, or much closer to home?

As rebellion threatens to shatter a fragile peace, Hannah's heart whispers that just maybe Max isn't dead and that he is calling her home. Can she trust her heart, or will she remain caught out of time, her destiny floating away like embers on a breeze?

Etched in Starlight

Hannah's Heirloom - Prequel

Maxentius - a Roman soldier fresh from the battlefields of Armenia, arrives to take command of the military outpost of Masada, Herod's isolated citadel in the Judaean desert. A seemingly mundane posting after years of warfare, Maxentius finds it more challenging to maintain a focused garrison than to face the wrath of the Parthians across a disputed frontier.

Hannah - a young Hebrew physician spends her days dealing with injuries from street brawls, deprivation, disease and loss. As her beloved Jerusalem plunges into chaos, her brother — who belongs to a band of rebels determined to drive out their Roman occupiers — tells her of their plans to storm a desert fortress and steal the weapons stored there, persuading his reluctant sister to go with him.

Masada - following the ambush, Hannah finds and treats three badly wounded Roman soldiers. In the aftermath and against impossible odds, Hannah and Maxentius realise that they are more than healer and captive, their fate already etched in starlight.

Prelude to Fate

For Lucia, staring into the jaws of an horrific death, escape seems impossible.

Rufius Atellus, a veteran Roman soldier, is appalled when he recognises one of the victims about to be executed. Surely this is a ghastly mistake?

A ferocious she-wolf, anticipating a tasty meal, suddenly finds herself under a human's control.

In an unexpected twist, and as danger threatens, the lives of all three become inextricably entwined.

Was it chance brought them together in that theatre of bloodshed, or simply a prelude to fate?

Legacy of Flame and Ash
A Hannah's Heirloom Story

An unremarkable family ring — lost when its owner was killed in the catastrophic eruption of Vesuvius — is excavated after nearly two millennia buried under tons of pumice and ash, setting off an extraordinary sequence of events.

A brazen robbery, and the ring is lost again. The theft and subsequent investigation, inspire twelve-year-old Cristiano Rossi to dedicate his life to the search and recovery of stolen artefacts.

Fast forward twenty years. Whispers of a rare item being offered for sale on the black market, initiates a joint operation between the Italian and British branches of the, colloquially named, Art Squad.

Hannah Vallier and her tech savvy assistant, Bryony Emerson — whose abilities to track down the untraceable, led to them assisting the UK Art and Antiquities Unit — have unearthed an intriguing thread. Reluctantly, Cristiano agrees to team up with the pair to thwart the traffickers, retrieve the artefact and, hopefully, dismantle the site.

What ought to be a routine assignment is complicated by a rogue operative, an unexpected romance, an ancient connection, and a *very* angry ghost!

A Guardian Unexpected

The Nettleby Trilogy: Book One

August 1914: Europe is on the brink of catastrophe. In a small village in rural Lincolnshire, a wife kisses her husband goodbye.

Childhood sweethearts, Eliza and Joe have only been married two years. They could not have imagined how soon they would be torn apart by war, nor that the most unexpected of guardians would offer them hope during their darkest hours.

Under the Clock

The Nettleby Trilogy: Book Two

England 1908: Under the clock, on a sleepy station platform nestled in rural Lincolnshire, an unexpected romance blossoms.

Maisie: Every Friday, at precisely five to six, a handsome young man arrives at the station. I know the time because I can see the clock. The train pulls in, punctual as always, and among the alighting passengers is an elderly gentleman. The young man greets him with a smile and a handshake, then tucks his arm through the older man's and they leave the platform.

Every Friday.

Occasionally, we exchange a glance or two and, to be fair, I suspect I notice him more than he notices me.

Fred: I count the hours until Friday afternoon comes around. Not only because this marks the start of the weekend but also, and more importantly, I get to see the flower girl. I am clueless as to her name, yet my heart begins to race the minute the station comes into view. I almost run up the steps onto the platform, hoping for a glimpse of her bright smile.

Every Friday.

I doubt she ever notices me. I'm just a village lad, one more faceless person in the throng.

Then again, you never know what might happen… in an innocuous corner of a quiet platform…

…under the clock

Evie's War

with Rori Bleu

World War II catapulted ordinary people into extraordinary service to save the world from an insidious evil... even if that meant being forced to do things which, under normal circumstances, would be considered abhorrent.

Genevieve Rousseau, Evie to a select few, was one such person who could not escape this fate. Despite her covert endeavours to liberate Paris from the Germans, she finds herself labelled a collaborator and an enemy of the French Republic.

Her only hope of vindication lies in helping a dangerously handsome American, with questionable motives, to uncover the Germans' final revenge.

Could struggling to resist Major Jack Donovon prove to be the decisive battle in Evie's War?

Vindicta

with Rori Bleu

Nightmares come in many guises... but usually fade with the dawn...

Not so for Bobbi Jo Fletcher. A witness to the massacre of her family, she had to escape the murderers in the middle of the worst blizzard in centuries... and she was only 5!

Fast forward twelve years and Bobbi Jo dreams of starting a new life away from the trauma of her past and the antipathy of pitiless relatives.

The nightmare isn't over... but perhaps the tables have turned...

Vindicta - when death isn't retribution enough...

Regency Romance

Once Upon An Earl
Linen and Lace - Book One

When Fate saw fit to intervene in the life of Giles Trevallier, the very respectable Earl of Winchester, by dropping a female — soaked to the skin and with no memory of who she is or how she came to be there — literally at his feet, no one could have predicted the outcome.

While uncovering her identity, Giles realises he is falling hopelessly in love with his mystery guest, who unbeknownst to him, is succumbing to similar emotions; but, when the heart is involved, a thoughtless word or gesture can thwart even Fate's best-laid plans.

Faced with misunderstandings, whispers of scandal, secret documents and foreign agents, their chance at a happy ever after seems elusive, but fairy tales often happen when least expected, and love — however inconvenient — usually finds a way to conquer all.

To Unlock Her Heart
Linen and Lace - Book Two

Abused by a duke, and shunned by Society, relief seems at hand when Grace Aldeburgh is bequeathed a house in a small village, far from malicious gossips.

Once there, a tentative friendship blooms between Grace and Theo Elliott, the local doctor, who has already resolved to be the man to unlock her heart.

Just when happiness appears to be within her grasp, her erstwhile tormentor once again stalks Grace. After a failed kidnap attempt, the duke's quest culminates in an acrimonious confrontation, and the reason for his venal pursuit becomes agonisingly clear.

Love on a Winter's Tide

Linen and Lace - Book Three

Every day, Helena disappears into a world few acknowledge, helping the poor, downtrodden, and abused. A husband is the last thing she can be bothered with.

Busy managing his shipping line, Hugh Drummond sees no need for a wife, whose only joy is dancing and frivolity. If — and it was a huge if — he ever married, it would be to a woman as capable as he, not some giddy society Miss.

Then, Hugh meets Helena and despite their resolve, fate, it seems, has other ideas. As their attraction deepens however, treachery threatens to tear them apart. Will they uncover the perpetrator in time, or will their love be swept away, lost forever on a winter's tide?

A Love Unquenchable

Linen and Lace - Book Four

Jessica Drummond, a bright and cheerful young woman, rarely gives romance, let alone love, a thought. Long hours working in her brother's shipping office affords little chance of her ever meeting an eligible bachelor.

Duncan Barrington, veteran of the Napoleonic Wars, believes himself wounded in both body and soul. He has no intention of inflicting his demons on anyone, certainly not a beautiful and, in his opinion, irresponsible city lady.

One cold and snowy morning, the plight of a bedraggled puppy throws Jessica and Duncan together and, as a spark of something indefinable yet wholly unquenchable begins to burn, it is unclear who rescued whom.

A Hidden Rose

Linen and Lace - Book Five

After witnessing his mother's grief at the loss of his father, Nick Drummond resolved never to cause someone he loved such distress. Even the happiness of his siblings would not sway him — until he met Rose.

Rose Archer was almost content assisting her doctor father in a tiny fishing village in the north of Yorkshire. To experience the world beyond, a tantalising dream — until she met Nick.

Unexpectedly, the impossible becomes possible, and the renounced — desired above all things, but the shipwreck that brought them together, may yet tear them apart. Will Nick learn to trust his heart, or will his love for Rose remain forever hidden

The Daffodil Garden

Horrifically scarred during the war, William Harcourt - Marquis of Blackthorne - prefers to spend his days in the quiet of his daffodil garden; plants do not pity, turn away, or judge.

Lucy Truscott, whose life is far removed from that of the *ton*, has no idea that by saving the life of a young woman, to whom she bears an uncanny resemblance, her own will be placed in mortal danger.

A chance encounter leads to something more. William begins to trust that Lucy sees the man beneath the scars, while Lucy is persuaded that love might actually transcend status.

Unfortunately, before their courtship has really begun, someone has every intention of ending it - permanently.

The Unconventional Duchess

Refusing to suffer the humiliation of her husband flaunting his mistress at Society events, the newly married Duchess of Wallingstead, Ella Lennox, takes control of her life. She leaves London for the family's country seat in remote Yorkshire.

A woman alone, Ella spends the next four years turning a cold, grim house into a home, and transforming the fortunes of the estate. Not afraid of hard work, she soon earns the respect of those around her with her determination and unconventional attitude.

Out of the blue, the duke arrives. Resigned to another arduous visit, Ella is stunned when it seems he is attempting to court her.

Impossible!

Could her dream of a happy marriage be about to come true?

Everything hangs on a snowstorm, a herd of cows and an uninvited guest!

Rescuing Her Knight

The *de Wiltons* — Book One

A story, invented to keep a little girl distracted, marks the beginning of another tale. One destined to remain unfinished for twenty years.

At thirteen, Adam Marchmain became Kitty de Wilton's 'Knight of the Garden' — a title bestowed following an accident which resulted in six-year-old Kitty having her knee sutured. Kitty never forgot his gallantry, but pledges made as children rarely survive into adulthood.

Their paths separated until Fate decreed, they meet again.

Widowed, badly disfigured and his sight ruined, Adam returns to his family home, a shadow of his former self.

Similarly afflicted, although her scars are invisible, Kitty — against her better judgement — is persuaded to help Adam banish his demons. This requires a subterfuge which, if discovered, might shatter more than the bonds of friendship forged two decades previously.

To Kitty, determined to break through the shield Adam has erected, the risk is worth it.

To see his smile and hear his laughter.

To rescue the knight of her childhood.

Just when a fairy tale ending is within her grasp, Kitty is threatened by the man who murdered her husband. In a cruel twist the tables are turned, and Kitty is the one who needs rescuing.

Elusive Hearts

An Unexpected Romance — Book One

What happens when two people whose elusive hearts fight an indefinable attraction, neither looked for nor desired, dare to dream?

When her fiancé and sister abscond to Gretna Green on her wedding day, Sapphira Beresford longs to escape, to avoid the gossipmongers gloating over her misfortune. Disillusioned, she is determined not to be burnt again, swearing off romance and marriage.

A fortuitous invitation sees her embarking on a journey to Pompeii where she meets Leofwin Colleville, reclusive marquis, amateur antiquarian, and her host for the duration.

Although enamoured of the ruins gradually being unearthed and ecstatic to have the opportunity to assist, Sapphira is troubled by her host's attitude, which blows hot and cold.

A confirmed bachelor, Leofwin Colleville is happiest surrounded by ancient ruins, and would prefer to brave the whole of Napoleon's armies alone, than face a lady on the hunt for a husband. The arrival of an unexpected guest throws his unencumbered existence into turmoil, but the harder he strives to maintain his distance, the more she gets under his skin.

Sparks fly and, as Leofwin's truculence undermines Sapphira's already battered confidence, her adventure of a lifetime seems doomed to disaster.

Until the day she runs afoul of greedy treasure hunters.

In the aftermath what was scorned becomes the one thing they crave above all else, but when it comes to the heart, nothing is ever simple.

His Fiery Hoyden

A Novella

Livvy has no respect for the nobility; they let her down when she most needed them. Why should she accede to their demands now?

Philip, Lord Harrington, is stunned to discover the young heir to the dukedom lives a stone's throw away in a ramshackle cottage, and resolves to restore the child to his birthright.

They meet in a clash of wills, but just when it seems Livvy might surrender, the victory Philip desires, may not taste all that sweet.

A Regency Duet

Luck be a Pirate

Luck wasn't something retired pirate Kennet Alexson believed in — good or bad. However, even he had to concede that landing a job at Trentams shipyard, and meeting Lynette Collins, was more than coincidence.

Fortune it seemed, was smiling on him for once.

As Kennet adjusts to life on dry land, his friendship with Lynette deepens into something far more enduring, and what once seemed elusive now becomes possible.

Unfortunately, fate has other plans, and Kennet's good luck is about to run out.

The Highwayman's Kiss

Surrendered Hearts — Book One

Nothing exciting had ever happened to Juliette St Clair. Her days were spent assisting her father or calling on friends, wandering art galleries, taking constitutionals or, and more preferably, escaping into her books. Her evenings her evenings — an endless round of balls, where she preferred to remain invisible.

Until the day she was robbed by a highwayman.

A Regency Christmas Double

Heart Rescued

Four years since Jasper lost the woman he was hoping to marry. Four years since he closed his heart and withdrew from Society. He has no idea his reclusive existence is about to be shattered.

Enter his sister's best friend, Harriet, a flame haired beauty, who needs his help.

Reluctantly he agrees and as they spend time together, it is clear their feelings run deep. Although Harriet affects Jasper in a way no woman ever has, he believes her to be out of his league ~ but it's Christmas and she might just be the one to melt his frozen heart

Catch a Snowflake

Romance often blossoms in the most unlikely of places - but in a ward full of wounded soldiers - surely not?

When Lucas Withers comes face to face with Jemima Parsons - a young woman who blames him for her brother's injury - falling in love is the last thing on their minds. What neither of them anticipated, was the magic of snowflakes.

Fate is Curious

A Novella

Happily, ever after? No such thing! Bereft, following her beloved husband's sudden death, Lady Charlotte Sherbrooke has lost her belief in romantic nonsense.

Successful shipping merchant, Zacharie Romain, is no stranger to loss; his business can be hazardous. Moreover, his wife died in childbirth and even though it happened a decade ago, he has no mind to expose himself to such sorrow again.

They meet in less than joyful circumstances but, as the year turns and grief diminishes, the woes of a small boy become the catalyst for something wholly unexpected. Can Charlotte and Zacharie trust what Fate has in store or will past heartbreak prevent them from taking a chance on love?

A Christmas Prayer

with Ashlee Shades

A Short Story

An entreaty from a frightened child.

Orphaned and only nine, Caroline Thorne has to grow up before her time. She is doing everything she can to keep what is left of her family together and out of the workhouse but is terrified her prayers are not being heard. Or maybe they are…

A petition from a woman desperate for a family.

A chance meeting with three orphaned siblings, tugs at Elizabeth Barrington's heart strings. Thus far, she and her husband have not been blessed with children and, as Christmas approaches, a plan begins to form - one which might just be the answer to her prayers.

Two Christmas prayers, as different as they are the same.

Will they hear and, more importantly, heed the answer?

The Lady's Wager

Surrendered Hearts - Book Two

A Novelette

Ged Mowbray will do anything to avoid being married off to the suitable prospects his parents insist on parading in front of him.

Melissa Bouchard is under no illusion her sizeable dowry is the attraction to suitors, not her.

An overheard conversation leads to an offer too good to refuse, but what happens when a lady's wager, becomes a gamble on the happily ever after, you did not even realise you wanted?

Winning Emma

Surrendered Hearts - Book Three

A Novelette

Randolph Craythorpe — earl, covert operative, and occasional highwayman — believed his dalliance with Lady Felicity Hartwich would lead to marriage. It did, but not to him! The arrival of an unwelcome guest, however, provides the perfect opportunity to indulge in a little retaliation.

Emma Newbury accompanies her cousin, Lady Charity Anscombe, to London for the Christmas season. Once there, she comes face to face with the three men who witnessed the humiliating aftermath of her father's disgrace — one of whom, to her irritation, has taken up residence in her dreams.

Their infrequent encounters only serve to confuse but, while winter tightens its grip on the city, what was inconceivable becomes the one thing for which they both yearn, yet bound by Society's rules, cannot admit.

As the snow falls, Randolph begins to understand that to win Emma, he will have to surrender.

A Love Impossible

A Regency M/M Novelette

Tasked with investigating a heinous crime, Edward Lindsay travels from London to Dublin — a city which holds too many memories — in the guise of guardian to his sister. He knew it could be hazardous, and relished the challenge, but that wasn't what caused his stomach to tighten as they approached landfall.

Dublin held more than just a murderer.

There was also Aidan.

While attending a party, Aidan Griffen is astonished when he comes face to face with a man who fled Dublin two years previously. A man he has desperately tried to forget.

As Edward closes in on his quarry, a fire, deliberately extinguished, is rekindled. But what of it? Edward and Aidan share a love impossible, and to acknowledge their feelings — more dangerous than confronting a killer.

Is there any hope of a happily ever after?

Unravelling Roana

A Regency Novelette

Tired of being ignored by her husband, Roana Dumont, Countess of Brooketon does the one thing guaranteed to get his attention. She runs away… to Venice, leaving behind a set of riddles for him to solve… *if* he feels their marriage is worth saving.

Gideon Dumont, 6th Earl of Brooketon is flabbergasted when he discovers his wife has apparently vanished off the face of the earth. A series of puzzles, the only clue as to her whereabouts.

The question is… will he unravel them?

Love Kindled

A Regency Novelette

Recently widowed, Amelia Ingram - Countess of Gresham, decides to shake off the fetters from her arranged and loveless marriage. Exploiting her new-found independence, Amelia indulges her yearning to explore - incognito.

Her ploy works so well, she receives an offer of employment from the dangerously handsome, Rupert Latimer - Earl of Badlesmere. On impulse, she accepts and finds herself governess to Cate, a delightful scamp of a child. What began as a bit of a game on Amelia's part, evolves into something far more profound, and a flame she presumed impossible to ignite, is kindled.

An unexpected turn of events leads to yet another offer. This time there is far more at stake and, determined history not repeat itself, Amelia confesses her ruse.

Rupert has been burnt once. Will he douse the spark, or take a risk and trust his heart?

Fairy Tale Romance

Chasing Bluebells

A Fairy Tale Novella

Once upon a time, somewhere in France, there was a man whose reckless obsession led him down a dark path — one which, ultimately, cost him his life.

That ought to have been the end of it.

Regrettably, as is so often the case, those who least deserve it, suffer for the actions of others.

A decade after being sent away, Sebastien Daviau returns to the little village where everything began. Hoping to lay the ghosts of his childhood to rest, he studiously ignores the possibility, he might run into Charlotte de Montbeliard.

As luck would have it, Charlotte is the one who runs into him… well, his horse… and although the brief encounter leaves a lasting impression, neither recognises the other.

A name revealed causes a freak accident, catapulting Sebastien's past into his present, and bringing him face to face with a man whose reputation would intimidate the most ardent of suitors.

Can whatever is blossoming between Charlotte and Sebastien survive the challenge imposed, or is their happily ever after about to fade as quickly as the bluebells they loved to chase?

Contemporary Romance

Of Ruins and Romance

Kassandra Winters has intrigued Gabriel St Germain since he accidentally knocked her flying outside her university professor's office. Her face haunts his dreams, yet he never expected to see her again. So, he is surprised when she appears, as though destined to do so, in the middle of a ruin, and he concocts a plan to win her heart.

Gabriel's old-fashioned courtship touches something deep inside Kassie and, although struggling to believe someone as handsome as Gabriel could possibly be interested in her, she soon realises she has fallen irrevocably in love with him. However, just as Kassie shares everything of herself with Gabriel, her world comes crashing down.

Can their romance survive, or will it fall in ruins, like the relics of antiquity that brought them together?

All At Once It's You

When Alex arrives in the small village of Rosedale Abbey, to take up a position as a research assistant for a renowned archaeologist, the last thing she is looking for, or expects to find, is love.

Jake was perfectly happy with the status quo. When it came to relationships, he didn't do committed or long term. He called the shots, and if his current flame didn't like it, she knew what to do. A philosophy, which served him well - until he met Alex.

Romance blooms, but even as the untamed wilderness of the North

Yorkshire moors weaves its spell, a long-buried secret might yet jeopardise their happily ever after.

Cobweb Dreams

A Novella

A holiday on the Scottish isle of Mull was just the break Chloe Shepherd needed, an escape from her boring office job and her complete lack of anything resembling a social life. Romance, it seems, isn't on the cards and, although Chloe dreams of finding her soulmate she is beginning to believe love is like cobwebs — spun overnight, only to vanish in the early morning breeze.

Under sufferance, Dominic Winters makes a flying visit to Mull to check on a rental property owned by his family. He hasn't got time for this — so indulging in a holiday fling is the last thing on his mind.

A lamb stuck in a bog proves a most unexpected matchmaker and, while Mull weaves its magic, Chloe wonders whether those fragile cobwebs might be far more stubborn than she thought.

Just One Step

A Short Story

In the aftermath of an horrific car accident, Daisy Forrester travels to Italy - hoping, so far from her memories, she might begin to heal.

Archaeologist, and single father, Adam Willoughby is too busy looking after his young daughter to give romance let alone love, a thought.

Neither expects a chance encounter in an ancient ruin to be anything more, but sometimes, that's all it takes.

His Heart's Second Sigh

A Novella

Reuben Faulkner and Paige Latimer are two happily single people, who have no desire to upset the status quo.

Unexpectedly, they are thrown together, only to discover both want far more than a casual friendship.

Just when things take an interesting turn, Reuben's past catches up with them, and threatens to derail their blossoming romance before it has chance to start.

Dystopian Romance

Echoes & Illusions

The Hunters - Book 1

Twenty years after a global plague, the remnants of civilisation struggle to eke out an existence in a world where humanity is secondary to survival.

On the outskirts of a once vibrant Rome, Gabriel tends his vineyard. From dawn to dusk, he strives to carve out a living, while caring for Bianca, his heavily pregnant wife.

Life might be tough, but at least he had an income, meagre though it was. Trouble seemed a distant memory, until the day he notices their neighbours are not at work in the adjacent fields.

A gruesome discovery sparks a chain of events to rival the conflicts Rome witnessed at the height of its power. Gabriel and Bianca must pit their wits and their lives against a formidable opponent, in an attempt prevent an atrocity none could have predicted.

A bond, forged in a snowy field and strengthened in a city under siege, is put to the ultimate test.

In a world of echoes and illusions, is their love strong enough to surmount the odds, or will it crumble to dust like the empire their enemies are striving to replicate?

Printed in the USA
CPSIA information can be obtained
at www.ICGtesting.com
LVHW022144161024
794041LV00025B/466